VOICES

FROM THE

BITTER CORE

VOICES

FROM THE

BITTER CORE

URSULA KRECHEL

TRANSLATED FROM THE GERMAN BY
AMY KEPPLE STRAWSER

HOST PUBLICATIONS

AUSTIN, TX

Host Publications, Inc. 277 Broadway, Suite 210, New York, NY 10007

Layout and Design: Joe Bratcher & Anand Ramaswamy
Cover Photo: Leonor Beuter
Jacket Design: Anand Ramaswamy

First Edition

Library of Congress Cataloging-in-Publication Data

Krechel, Ursula, 1947-
[Stimmen aus dem harten Kern. English]
Voices from the bitter core / Ursula Krechel ; translated from the German by Amy Kepple Strawser.
    p. cm.
ISBN-13: 978-0-924047-65-7 (hardcover : alk. paper)
ISBN-10: 0-924047-65-8 (hardcover : alk. paper)
ISBN-13: 978-0-924047-66-4 (pbk. : alk. paper)
ISBN-10: 0-924047-66-6 (pbk. : alk. paper)
I. Strawser, Amy Kepple. II. Title.
PT2671.R383S7513 2009
831'.914--dc22
                        2008044998

TABLE OF CONTENTS

LETTING THE COMPLICIT SPEAK:
URSULA KRECHEL'S *VOICES FROM THE BITTER CORE*

When Ursula Krechel's *Stimmen aus dem harten Kern* appeared in 2005, the United States' post-September 11 invasions of Afghanistan and Iraq were still fresh in everyone's mind. As these conflicts endure into the present day, the timelessness of Krechel's long poem has not lessened. Indeed, its myriad voices—mainly soldiers, conquerors and occupiers—speak still with intensity and authenticity from many centuries and battlefields the world over.

Since she became an independent writer in 1972, Ursula Krechel has produced a rich and diverse body of work in the German-speaking realm. Yet this translation of *Stimmen aus dem harten Kern* heralds the first publication of a full-length book in English, a fact not easily explained or excused. Prominent in Europe primarily as a poet, Krechel has only recently received much long-deserved critical acclaim at home for *Shanghai fern von wo* (*Shanghai, Far From Everywhere*, 2008) through several prestigious literary prizes—the Joseph-Breitbach and the German Critics' Awards, among others. This novel, a tour-de-force of prose fiction, explores in depth the experiences of German and Austrian Jewish refugees in that city in China on the cusp of the Holocaust, based on several decades of extensive research, interviews and travel.

Krechel's oeuvre continues to reveal and unravel intricacies of thought, feeling, and poetic structure unrivaled among her contemporaries. Her early work coincided with the rise of women's literature and feminist criticism, along with the advent of the *Neue Subjektivität* (*New Subjectivity*) in German letters. Several early volumes of poetry, along with her first published literary work, the play *Erika* (1973), handle themes from a distinctly female perspective. However, a wide-ranging aesthetic as well as a broad legacy of intellectual and literary history inform and underlie her writing, defying any attempt to easily classify it. At times, Krechel's poetry has even tended towards the abstract and esoteric, such as the volume *Vom Feuer lernen* (*Learning from Fire*, 1985), which, like *Voices*, interweaves into the poems elements of borrowed texts whose origins are mentioned in an appendix, though without precise annotations.

In the present volume, the poet has gathered authentic texts from sources as diverse as Mussolini, Rimbaud, Stephen Spender, Ernst Toller and Georg Trakl, and woven their words into poetic segments alongside the thoughts and feelings of ordinary foot soldiers, trench-dwellers and ethnic-cleansers—those young men who do the dirty work of their superiors, those carrying out orders from above. Questions remain: Who takes responsibility? Who is guilty? The text provides no easy answers.

The preeminence of violence, whether explicit or implied, in how humans interact with one another could not be more clearly stated or evident than we find here. This is a male-centered universe, and only a handful of female figures appear throughout the entire long poem—still fewer speak—mostly present for the sexual gratification of the men or as the victims of other atrocities. Krechel evinces a multifaceted portrait of war's anti-heroes and perpetrators, in particular, those everyday fighters who do not make the history books.

Krechel has given voice to those involved in the business of war-making who are normally silent or silenced. They are, for the most part, neither politicians nor generals nor conscripted warriors; they willingly take part and play out their role with varying degrees of both eagerness and trepidation. As readers, we gain insight into the machinations of the military dynamic, from the inside out and the bottom up. These tough guys pay gravely with body and soul. Krechel has, in *Voices from the Bitter Core*, mastered the long poem with such precision, force and crystalline expression that the reading hits you like a stomach-punch and brings you to your knees.

—Amy Kepple Strawser
February, 2010

Voices from the Bitter Core quotes found materials,
assembles texts and textures, some are named here.

Heimrad Bäcker: "postscript 2." Graz/Vienna 1997 (IV, 12)

Viktor Jerofejew: "Preparation for the Orgy." *New Russian Literature.* Cologne 2000 (VI, 4, VI, 7)

Jochen Klepper: "Overcoming. Diaries and Notations from the War." Stuttgart 1958 (IV, 5, 6, 10)

Theodor Kramer: "We lay in Volhynia in the Swamp." (I, 12)

Benito Mussolini: "My War Diary." Zurich/Leipzig/Vienna 1930 (V, 2)

Arthur Rimbaud: Letter of November 17, 1878 to his family (V, 1)

Stephen Spender: "Germany in Ruins." Frankfurt 1998 (VIII, 6, 7, 10)

Ernst Stadler: Letter to Erwin Wissmann from October 3, 1914 (I, 6)

Ernst Stadler: "Beginning of Winter." (IV, 9)

Peter Szondi: "Experiment on the Tragic." Frankfurt 1961 (VIII, 5)

Ernst Toller: Letter from the Stadelheim prison to Maximilian Harden 1919. (VIII, 8)

Georg Trakl: "On Quiet Days." (XI)

"Censorship in the GDR. History, Praxis and the 'Aesthetics' of the Obstruction of Literature." Ed. Ernest Wichner and Herbert Wiesner. Berlin 1991, in it Joachim Seyppel: "The Porcelain Dog." (VI, 5, VI, 6).

AUTHOR'S NOTE

Voices from the Bitter Core is a long poem of twelve poetic sequences or stanzas [of twelve poems] of twelve lines each. It is thus a work of 12 times 12 times 12 verses. The regularity and strictness of the form speak to the violence of the text and relate to the violence of the topic, castigation by means of history. The voices that speak and are brought to speech in this poem cycle are invaders, colonizers, marauding troops and their victims, collectively the rubbed-bloody reverse side of the consciously articulate world, which retreats into reticence. The long poem follows the call of a fighting body of soldiers across historical epochs and myths. It listens to the sounds of decampment, sees traces of desolation and devastation in their minds. Why do they fight, why do men band together and follow orders? Must the description of a shield be considered the beginning of literature, or does the stench of a wound thrust itself into the foreground? This long poem is a radical portrait of a militant masculine condition shown through their words and objects, written also with the perception of how rapidly these can be recharged with new meanings and signifiers. Two figures—possibly surprising in their mirror image of each other—appear as individuals in one poetic sequence each: the wide-ranging poetic and politically-strategically thinking Lord Byron, to whom I once previously dedicated a poem in 1985, and the mythical figure of Philoctetes, whom Sophocles portrayed with his inner conflict and Heiner Müller as a has-been, failed combatant. I am interested in writing, thinking about the formidable continuum of the imperial, about the armament and disarmament [building up and tearing down] of a battery of words, about its amalgamation in economic processes. (See section IX)

A brief literary-historical consideration: The long poem as poetic object should be differentiated from the epic poem in terms of its structure and characteristic of epoch-making. The epic poem narrates, explains, interprets the world. The long poem creates its own subject matter: see [Anna] Akhmatova, "Poem without a Hero"; T.S. Eliot, *The Waste Land*; Hart Crane, *The Bridge*. The long poem is a large form of the poem, chopped up, assembled, and it is distinct from a poetic tale in verse.

—Ursula Krechel

VOICES

FROM THE

BITTER CORE

I

Motivation

Orakeldeutung

Meine Herren, die Intelligenz und Phantasie der Leute hat sich darin zu zeigen, daß man den Blitz einfängt. Ich versichere Ihnen, ich zum Beispiel lebe nur, weil ich mich mir suggeriere; in Wirklichkeit bin ich tot.

Carl Einstein: Bebuquin oder Die Dilettanten des Wunders

I

Motivation

Interpretation of the Oracle

Gentlemen, the intelligence and imagination of the people are made clear by the fact that one captures lightning. I assure you I, for example, live only because I suggest myself to me; in reality, I am dead.

Carl Einstein: Bebuquin or the Dilettantes of Miracles

1

Tatsache ist: Wir haben den Peloponnesischen Krieg nicht begonnen
Scharmützel, alles auf eine Karte, Beschreibung eines Schildes

Gewiß: wir haben mit dem Peloponnesischen Krieg nichts am Hut
Und als Troja brannte, waren wir nachweislich über alle Berge

Der Krieg ist uns aufgezwungen worden von solchen, die leicht=
Fertig unsere Gegner werden wollten am Rand der bewohnten Welt

Erde verbrannt haben sie selbst angerichtet, Köder ausgelegt, das Hemd
Aufgeschlitzt, damit die nackte Brust, das nackte Mitleid sich paaren

Wir haben Opfer gebracht, um uns selbst nicht unglückselig zu opfern
Als Opfer unserer zukünftigen Gegner, die sich zu spät formierten

Und dringen in rechtsfreie Räume vor in geordneten Textverbänden
Wollen beschrieben (besungen?) werden, damit wir schweigen können.

1

Fact is: We did not begin the Peloponnesian War
Skirmish, all eggs in one basket, description of a shield

Certainly: the Peloponnesian War was not our cup of tea
And as Troy burned, we were undeniably miles away

The war has been forced upon us by those who care –
Freely wanted to be our enemies at the ends of the earth

Soil scorched they arranged themselves, laid out bait, the shirt
Slit open, so that the bare breast, naked mercy mate

We have made sacrifices in order not to sacrifice ourselves haplessly
As the victims of our future enemies who formed up too late

And penetrate into lawless regions in classified text collectives
Want to be described (sung about?) so that we can be silent.

2

Alle waren entschlossen zum Krieg, was sehr begreiflich war
Am Anfang faßte jeder gern schärfer an, wetzte die Zunge

Damals schwappte viel Jugend in die Peloponnes und nach Athen
Die in ihrer Unerfahrenheit freudig jede Neuigkeit aufgriff

Prognosen waren in aller Munde, Spatzen pfiffen, Orakeldeuter
Hatten gute Konjunktur, ein sanftes Erdbeben rüttelte uns durch

Das wenig beschädigte, aber als Hoffnungszeichen des Himmels
Gedeutet – seit Menschengedenken gab's das nicht zu Beginn

Kein Herold, kein Bote sollte empfangen werden, keine Irritationen
Zucht, Wachsamkeit hießen die Tugenden, derer wir uns altmodisch

Befleißigten, so wuchsen wir über uns hinaus glaubwürdig heldisch
Waren wir uns unser selbst gewiß und unserer Waffensysteme.

2

All were determined to go to war, which was very understandable
At first everyone joined in enthusiastically, whetted the tongue

At that time many youths swashed into Peloponnesus and to Athens
Who in their inexperience gladly seized every piece of news

Predictions were on every tongue, sparrows tweeted, prophets
Had good business, a gentle earthquake shook us up

Which damaged little but was construed as a sign of hope from
Heaven – according to living memory that did not exist from the start

No herald, no messenger was to be welcomed, no irritations
Breeding, vigilance were the virtues to which we outdatedly

Applied ourselves, thus we outgrew ourselves believably heroically
We were sure of ourselves and our weapon systems.

3

Unstete Reisen erweitern das Weltbild, wir aber, die Guten
Beweglich und wohl ausgestattet, Schlachtrösser und Helme

Pfeile und Speere, nicht zu vergessen die Minen und Sprengsätze
Heisere Hunde liefen uns nach, sie rochen Blut, Schweiß etc.

Vormarsch, Invasion, vereinzelte Motorengeräusche aus
Einer unausdenkbaren Zeit, die als ein Nachtschatten über uns

Erfinderische Zukunft, in der Plastiktüten auf Bäumen wachsen
Und Leute wie wir ausgedehnte Reisen in silbernen Kisten

Weit weg, wo anderswo in Jurten Milch floß und Honig
Während uns ein Stahlgewitter blüht, vibrierende Drähte

Setzten uns in Bewegung Meldegänger Kolonnen Landenge
Und stolz in einem einzigen Wummtata unsere Verbündeten.

3

Unsteady journeys expand the horizon, but we, the good ones
Mobile and well equipped, battle steeds and helmets

Arrows and spears, not to mention the mines and the explosives
Hoarse dogs ran after us, they smelled blood, sweat, etc.

Advance, invasion, isolated sounds of engines from
An unthinkable time like a nightshade over us

Imaginative future, where plastic bags grow on trees
And people like us lengthy journeys in silver boxes

Far away, where elsewhere in yurts milk flowed and honey
While for us a storm of steel blossoms, vibrating wires

Set us in motion harbingers convoys isthmus
And proud in a single oom pah pah our allies.

4

Beiderseits rüstet man zum großen Schlage, den zu vermeiden
Unmöglich. Mama ist immer noch in Badenweiler, schickt

Tee und getrocknete Früchte. Gegenwart: stumpf und blind
Und ich bin Gefreiter, taugl., warum rücken wir vor, ohne uns

Um die schönen Aprikosenbäume, die Siedlungen, Zeltlager
Zu kümmern, das zuckende Herz zu verbergen, solange wir

Vorrücken, uns nicht vergraben, Einsamkeit kalt wie Fensterglas
Ist die Rückseite der Kameraderie, wir kennen Streitwagen und

Bataillone, Kohorten, Artillerie, Uniformknöpfe und Tanks
Zünden ein großes Feuer an, auch Sonne begrüßt uns taggrell

In den Unterständen wird geraucht, gesungen und geschrieben
Auf der Veranda sitzen Offiziere, trinken stark gesüßten Kaffee.

4

On both sides they prepare for the great coup, impossible
To avoid. Mama is still in Badenweiler, sends

Tea and dried fruit. Present time: dull and blind
And I am a private, fit, why are we advancing, without

Tending the beautiful apricot trees, the colonies, tent camps
Hiding the pounding heart, as long as we advance,

Don't bury ourselves, loneliness cold like window glass
Is the reverse of camaraderie, we know chariots and

Battalions, cohorts, artillery, uniform buttons and tanks
Ignite a large fire, also sun greets us glaring as day

In the dugouts they are smoking, singing and writing
On the veranda sit officers, drink strongly sweetened coffee.

5

Bei Tagesanbruch: „Erster Zug aufpacken." Wir steigen
Auf Hänge, die abgeholzt worden sind für unsere Flotte

Haine aus Eichen vormals, Pinien, glorreiches Waldmoos
Wir steigen ausgetrocknete Bachläufe entlang, Geröllhalden

Wir steigen im Schattenlosen, Waldbrandgefahr über uns
Vogelschwärme, die niemand zu deuten sich die Zeit nimmt

Gute Sicht auf dornige Sträucher, auf Beine des Vordermanns
Wir steigen wie Maultiere und sind doch Göttersöhne oder

Ihnen ähnlich, uns glückt das Beginnen, wie weiter beginnen
Wenn jeder Befehl möglichst „wörtlich" auszuführen ist

Wir steigen in die triumphal heimgeführte Geschichte auf
Die zu schreiben dem späteren Heeresberichterstatter obliegt.

5

At dawn: "Pack up the first platoon." We climb
Onto slopes which were deforested for our fleet

Groves of oak in former times, pines, glorious wood moss
We climb along dried up stream currents, rubble heaps

We climb without shade, danger of forest fire above us
Swarms of birds which no one takes the time to interpret

Good view of thorny bushes, of legs of the man in front
We climb like mules and still are sons of the gods or

Like them, we are lucky at the start, how to continue
If every command is to be followed as "literally" as possible

We ascend into the triumphal home-led history
That must be written as a future official communiqué.

6

Was begann, konnten wir nicht einmal „Krieg" nennen, eher
Ungestört unruhige Nacht oder vorschnell fixe Kameraderie

Wir bemerkten auch Schwarzmaler, die nie eine Schlacht
Von hinten und vorn gesehen hatten, wir nannten, was nicht

Zu benennen war, auch Angst oder Zeitläufte, die historisch
Unser Nachtlager war der Keller eines fast gastlichen Hauses

Das genügte fürs erste, wir waren zufrieden, daß etwas geschah
Mit uns und mit dem Gegner, den wir nicht wirklich verstanden

Über die allgemeine Lage wissen wir wenig, aber das macht
Nichts, wir befinden uns passabel, werden weidlich beschossen

Entgegnen das Feuer. Zur Verheiratung die herzlichsten Wünsche:
„Vor ein paar Tagen habe ich das Eiserne Kreuzzeichen erhalten."

6

What began we couldn't even call "war," rather
Undisturbed restless night or hastily ready-made camaraderie

We also noticed doom-mongers who had never seen
A battle from the front or the back, we named what was

Not nameable, also fear or the passage of time which historically
Was our night camp the cellar of an almost hospitable house

That sufficed at first, we were satisfied that something happened
With us and with our enemy whom we didn't really understand

About the general situation we know little, but that doesn't
Matter, our situation is tolerable, we are shelled far and wide

Encounter the fire. For your marriage, warmest wishes:
"A few days ago I received the Iron Sign of the Cross."

7

Lehrbuch: jeder Befehl ist „möglichst wortwörtlich" auszuführen
Stellen sich unvorhersehbare Schwierigkeiten in den Weg

Darf der Soldat den Befehl, ein eingefleischtes Tun, nicht
Als unausführbar ansehen (Erl. zu KriegsArt. 11) vielmehr

Sehe er sich um in seinem Verstand, wie die Schwierigkeit
Zu überwinden. Vielleicht auf andere Weise ans Ziel oder

Hauptsache: Der Soldat hat den „Sinn" des Befehls begriffen
D.h. worauf es eigentlich ankommt, und er führt aus aus aus

Daher muß er eifrig bemüht sein, seine Pflichten zu erfüllen
Und erfüllt sein vom Befohlenwerden auf weite Sicht (Art. 1)

Man nennt dies „sinngemäße" automat. Ausführung eines Befehls
Wenn aber ein Befehl ausbleibt, weil der Befehlsgeber. Tusch.

7

Textbook: every command is to be carried out "as literally as possible"
If unforeseeable difficulties present themselves along the way

The soldier may regard the command, a flesh and blood
Deed, not as unfeasible (Expl. to War Art. 11) in fact

He should search his mind about how to resolve
The difficulty. Perhaps to reach the goal another way or

Essential: the soldier comprehends the "sense" of the command
I.e., what it really depends on, and he carries it out out out

Hence he must be avidly concerned with fulfilling his duties
And fulfilled with being commanded in a broad sense (Art. 1)

One automatically calls this "analogous." But following an order
When an order is absent because the commander. Flourish.

8

Um jederzeit aufgelegt schießen zu können, sind Ziel=
Stöcke konstruiert, über deren Benutzung kein Urteil

Erlauben sie doch auch weniger guten Kugelschützen
Ein sicheres Abkommen und manche Qual als Folge

Schlechter Schüsse ersparen sie. Sitzt der Schütze aber
Auf der Erde, aus guter Deckung die Kugel antragen

Ein geringer Druck, Sabotagefälle durch Brandstiftung
Sowie mutwillige Vernichtung von Material und Person –

Jedes Gewehr muß beim Nichtgebrauch gesichert werden
Sobald der Stecher so weit rückwärts gezogen im Ruck, daß

Ein Knacken hörbar (Rückstecher), zeigt der Sicherungsflügel
Nach rechts und ist ein Auslösen des Schusses ausgeschlossen.

8

To be prepared to shoot at any moment, sights
Are constructed, no judgment about their use

Yet they also allow those who are less good shots
An assured outcome and much pain as a result

Bad shots they spare. But if the shooter sits on the
Ground marking out the bullet from good cover

A slight pressure, cases of sabotage by means of arson
As well as willful destruction of materials and people –

Every gun must be secured when not in use
Once the pin is pulled so far back with a jerk that

A snap is audible (rear set trigger), the safety flank points
To the right and releasing the shot is impossible.

9

Wir schnitten dramatische Gesichter, wie harte Jungs sie haben
Kinnlade vorgeschoben und die Lippen strikt darüber gepreßt

Nur die Nüstern nehmen die Witterung auf, trockene Schleim=
Häute, Duldungsstarre, Rotz und Wasser sind vom anderen Ufer

Etwas malmt in den Kinnladen, kein Wort, die Kauflächen
Der Backenzähne pressen Begehrlichkeiten, kein Laut oder leis

Dringt aus dem geschlossenen Mund, Augen zu Schlitzen verengt
Und was wir gehört haben, Spektakel Orakel vergessen wir sofort

Wir sind Panzer, wir sind Truppentransporter, überaus verläßlich
Weitsichtig, gut ausgebildet (Schild und Schwert und Raketen)

Und unsere Gesichter erinnern von fern an stürmische Höhen
Kühle Himmelsverdunklungen, und wohin mit den Händen

Den lästigen

9

We made dramatic faces like tough boys have
Jaw thrust forward and lips sternly drawn above

Only the nostrils absorb the weather, dry mucous membranes
Numb from acquiescing, snot and water are from the other bank

Something is grinding in the jaws, not a word, the chewing surfaces
Of the molars squeeze hidden desires, not a sound or quietly

Forces out of the closed mouth, eyes narrowed to slits
And what we have heard, spectacles oracles we forget at once

We are tanks, we are troop carriers, extremely reliable
Farsighted, well trained (shield and sword and missiles)

And our faces are reminiscent from afar of stormy heights
Cool eclipses of the heavens, and what to do with our hands

Those cumbersome things

10

In Wirklichkeit brauchten wir unsere Hände gar nicht
Wir hatten Armaturen, auf denen mit einem Blick –

Es war fünf Uhr zweiunddreißig MEZ, wir schüttelten
Den Schlaf aus den Isoliermatten, die Mannschaftswärme

Ein träges Möbel, das wir mit Rasierschaum bepinselten
Unsere Kiefer durchpflügten Wasser in dünnen Rinnsalen

Nicht zum Verzehr geeignet, wir hatten Flaschen und Filter
Meerwasser aufbereitet, zerbissene Kaugummis in den Sand

Rückten wir vor, war eine Obstplantage regimetreu geblieben
Wir durchsiebten das Blätterdach, in dem wir Heckenschützen

Vermuteten. (Später falsifiziert.) Haus brannte, Aprikosen fielen
Zu Boden, niemand aß, niemand nahm Notiz vom Nichtessen.

10

In reality we didn't need our hands at all
We had instruments that with one look –

It was five thirty-two o'clock CET, we tossed
The sleep from the isolation mats, the team warmth

An inert piece of furniture we painted with shaving cream
Our jaws plowed through water in thin rivulets

Unfit for consumption, we had bottles and filters
Salt-water purified, bits of chewing gum in the sand

Did we advance, had a fruit plantation remained loyal
We screened the leaf roof where we suspected

Snipers. (Later unfounded.) House burned, apricots fell
To the ground, no one ate, no one noticed we weren't eating.

11

Weiße Blätter, das Chlorophyll herausgewaschen, nur die Adern
Noch zartgrün, und Spinnen, die ihre sanften Fäden zogen

Von Blatt zu Blatt, Verhandlungsstrategen in ihrem Netzwerk
Weiße Blätter gegen den harten Himmel, war das ein Zeichen

Das stillsteht jetzt im Angriff, während wir uns nähern (robben)
Was stillsteht jetzt im Schock, das Muskelherz, der Atemhauch

In der rauchgeschwärzten Luft seh ich die Fiedervögel fallen
War das ein Zeichen, ich vergaß es nicht, vergaß mich selbst

Ich war ein Zeichen, nur ein Ornament des Aufgebrochenwerdens
Des Gehens, Gegangenwerdens und Gegängeltwerdens, ich war

Ein weißes Blatt, herausgewaschen aus dem Blätterwald, segelte
Wohin was wußte ich was weiß der Wind, ich wartete auf mich

Nicht.

11

White leaves, the chlorophyll washed out, only the veins
Still tender-green, and spiders drew their gentle strands

From leaf to leaf, negotiation strategists in their network
White leaves against the grim sky, was that a sign

That now stops during the attack, while we converge (crawl)
What now stops in shock, the muscular heart, the respiration

In the smoke-blackened air I see the feathered birds fall
Was that a sign, I didn't forget it, forgot myself

I was a sign, merely an ornament of being decamped
Of going, having gone and being led by the nose, I was

A blank page, washed out of the forest of leaves, sailed
Where to what did I know what does the wind know, I waited

                                        Not for myself.

12

Und morgen die ganze Welt und übermorgen zur Teilnahme
Bewegen feindliche Truppenverbände leichte Reiter und Speere

Auf die gespießt – nicht auszudenken, wenn einem selbst jedoch
„Durchbohrten und töteten ihn", „in fremde Hände fallen" oder

Wie es im Heeresbericht hieß. Wir lagen in Wolhynien im Morast
Erwarteten den Anfang, die Mutter aller, die Hellebarden gespitzt

In den Zelten tropfte das Wasser, und ein eisiger Atem hauchte
Über die Ebene, rannten dem Ausgang zu, aber unbekannt dunkel

Sofort stoppten zwei Tanks, eine Tragbahre zerbrach, umladen, was
Mit blutigen Händen gelang. Einzelfall, Sturmangriff, abgewehrt

Lange Ermutigungsreden geschmettert. Vorteilhaft für den Krieg
Sei aber anderes: Beute, Rechtsansprüche. Und Ausradieren von.

12

And tomorrow the whole world and the next day to join in
Enemy troop formations move facile horsemen and spears

Skewering them – inconceivable if oneself however
"Pierced and killed him," "falls into enemy hands" or

As in the official report. We lay in Volhynia in the swamp
Anticipated the beginning, the mother of all, halberds sharpened

In the tents water dripped and an icy breath breathed
Across the plain, ran to the way out, but unknown dark

At once two tanks stopped, a stretcher broke, reload, which
Was managed with bloody hands. Isolated case, assault, averted

Long speeches of encouragement blared. Advantageous for the war
Would be something else: loot, legal claims. And obliteration of.

II

Konzentration

Vorrücken

II

Concentration

Advancing

1

Wir gehen aber nun schon sehr lange, „rücken vor"
Auf der Piste, sind eingenistet und schwer vergraben

Alles war Bartschatten, unerwidertes Sehen im Dunklen
Stehenbleiben wie gegangen werden und gebrandmarkt

Sind wir aber im Schatten ein einziges Einverständnis
Mit dem Befohlenen und haben uns gründlich eingeseift

Und Wörter wie Wasserspiegel, Sauerstoffkonzentration
(Die wir miteinander teilen) fielen unrühmlich ins Wasser

Stürmischer Sand und waren so übermäßig gegangen
Knietief und die Instrumente an Seilen über den Köpfen

Daß Erkenntnis von Wasserspiegel und Bewässerung
Als zwei Seiten einer Medaille nicht auseinanderklafften.

1

We have now been walking for a very long time, "advancing"
On the slope, are nestled in and deeply burrowed

Everything was five o'clock shadow, unrequited seeing in the dark
Standing still like being walked and being branded

Are we however in the shadow an exclusive agreement
With the commanded and have thoroughly duped ourselves

And words like sea level, oxygen concentration
(That we share with each other) ingloriously failed

Tempestuous sand and had walked so excessively
Knee-deep and the instruments on ropes above our heads

That realization of sea level and irrigation
Like two sides of a medal did not split apart.

2

Eindringen in weiches, ungeschütztes Gelände, aufgewühlte
Sandbänke und Pisten, die aussahen, als hätten sie nicht auf uns

Gewartet, manche von uns dachten an Frauen, Fleischliches, wir
Penetrierten die Peloponnes, rodeten Dattel- und Olivenbäume

Zündeten Feuer an, Reisig, Gestrüpp, Dornenzweige, auf denen
Fleischballen geschmort wurden, Luft stand still, zitterte trocken

Ich war einer, der in die Luft starrte mit stechenden Wimpern
Sie hielten die Sonne nicht ab. Versuchte mich historisch zu sehen

Fühlte mich klein wie ein Kieselstein, doch nicht so abgeschliffen
Ich dachte an viele von uns, die wie alle fühlten (Kloß in der Kehle)

Wir hörten Kolonnen, waren wir das, griffen wir an oder war
Keine Angriffsfläche im Sand, Ziegel fielen von den Dächern

Scherbengericht

2

Intruding into pliant, unprotected terrain, churned up
Sand banks and slopes that looked like they hadn't

Waited for us, some of us thought of women, things carnal, we
Penetrated the Peloponnesus, cleared out date and olive trees

Lit fires, brushwood, undergrowth, brambles upon which
Hunks of meat were braised, air stood still, shivered dry

I was one who stared into the air with stinging eyelashes
They didn't keep the sun out. Tried to view myself historically

Felt I was small as a pebble, although not so worn away
I thought about many of us who felt like everyone (lump in the throat)

We heard convoys, was that us, did we attack or were there
No target areas in the sand, bricks fell from the roofs

Ostracism

3

Was wir sahen im Sand, mußten wir Fußspuren nennen
Und wir nannten es so: „Fußspuren". Wir erfanden einen

Dem sie gehörten. Und wir nannten ihn „Feind" (gegnerisch)
Wir wußten, daß er da war, und wir waren da, ihn zu stellen

Wir stellten ihn uns vor im lichten Augenblick des Überraschtwerdens
Und überraschten uns selbst mit unserer blendenden Laune, die

Wir in Mikrophone pusteten. Wir nannten uns „wir", waren aber
Vereinzelt bis in die grauen Zellen und zogen uns zurück ins Innere

Der Augenwinkel (um die Körper Schlafsäcke, Anorakmontur)
Wir rieben die Rücken aneinander. „Überwältigen" war ein Wort

Das angemessen erschien wie „Kruppe", das wir aber nicht benutzten
Fiel aus dem Rahmen, den wir uns unfreiwillig gegeben hatten.

3

What we saw in the sand we had to call footprints
And we called them that: "footprints." We invented the one

To whom they belonged. And we called him "foe" (adversarial)
We knew that he was there, and we were there to engage him

We imagined him in the clear moment of being surprised
And surprised ourselves with our dazzling mood which

We blew into microphones. We called ourselves "we" but were
Isolated down to the gray cells and withdrew into the inside

Of the corners of our eyes (around our bodies sleeping bags, anorak garb)
We rubbed our backs against each other. "Overpower" was a word

That seemed appropriate, like "croup" that we however did not use
Went too far, something we had unintentionally allowed ourselves.

4

Ja, wir konnten uns mit allem identifizieren, Sonne ging auf
Mit düstrer Pracht, stieg bis Mittag, Luft und Granatapfelbaum

Kurze Belichtungszeiten, Zeichen der Bewegung (Gemüt, Gestüt)
Doch die Pferde scheu gemacht, um eines einzigen Satzes willen

Differenz zwischen der Einstellung und Intention, schließlich
Mit allem und jedem und keinem. Modell stand das Pferd

Die Nüstern, sein Schädel, das Brandmal, Zeit verschwand von
Der Bildfläche, die mit Fingerabdrücken übersät, wo die Augen

Entscheiden, Schlüsse wie Schlußfolgerungen und tägliches
Brot – natürlich hinkt der Vergleich: gib uns ein Zeichen.

Die Haut ist nicht Text, Pferdehaut vom Impuls her ähnlich
Wie weit man traben kann, dynamisch, ohne sich zu erübrigen.

4

Yes, we could identify with everything, sun came up
With dreary splendor, rose till midday, air and pomegranate tree

Short exposure times, signs of movement (mind, stud)
Yet the horses made shy for the sake of a single sentence

Deviation between the attitude and intention, ultimately
With everything and everyone and no one. The horse was posing

The nostrils, its skull, the brand, time disappeared from
The picture screen, littered with fingerprints, where the eyes

Decide, conclusions like argumentation and daily
Bread – of course the comparison is lame: give us a sign.

The skin is not text, similar to horse skin by the impulse
How far one can trot, dynamically, without being superfluous.

5

Sprunggelenk, aber nicht wirklich zum Aufbruch geeigenet
Vorgesehen für fiktives Springen, trainierte Muskelkraft

An Hecken, Schönheit, Belastungsfähigkeit minus Charme, wie
Die Flugbahn sich dem Objektiv verbündet, Lichteinfall und

Die Struktur der Haut perfekt zurückgeworfen, Fallschirmhaut
Der Glanz frisch gestriegelter Tiere, beispielhafte Verbindung

Oder Fehlfarben, falb, zurückgezüchtet bis zum Urpferd, das
Zum Leiblichkeitscharakter regelrecht mutiert, Züchtungserfolg

In vielen Armeen auftrumpft die Gegenwart: mutiert, passiert
Paßgang geschnellt, Paßgenauigkeit der Landung, Atemlosigkeit

Die auch ihre Berechtigung hat, dankbare Benutzer, Zeit
wahrt ihre Form, schwer bewaffnet. Empirischer Voyeurismus.

5

Ankle joint, but not really suitable for departure
Intended for virtual jumping, practiced muscle strength

On hedges, beauty, physical endurance minus charm, as
The flight path is aligned with the objective, incidence of light and

The structure of the skin perfectly reflected, parachute skin
The brilliance of freshly curried animals, exemplary connection

Or off-colors, dun, bred back to the primal horse that
Transforms properly to corporeal character, success in breeding

In many armies the present time brags: transformed, transpired
Pace sped up, precision of landing, breathlessness

That also has its justification, grateful operators, time
Keeps its shape, heavily armed. Empirical voyeurism.

6

Krieg ist auch ein Versuch, etwas in Erfahrung zu bringen
Das ohne Erfahrung zu Ende gebracht der Nacht dunkel

Geboten: dies ist auch ein Versuch, Worte zu machen, wo
Worte ohne Wurzeln, Stumpf und Stiel ausgerottet, doch

Nicht, wo Worte *crossover* gesetzt verpetzt gelassen aus
Ruhen schon die Wälder und dann die Stoppelfelder und

Fleisch gewordenes Verschweigen nur der Versuch, Herr
Zu werden ohne Beherrschungen, dargeboten im Tempel

Der ausgeräumt ausgeträumt aus dem Spiel: hier sind nur
Die Platzhalter, unselig unschuldig wissen sie von nichts

Gesetzt den Fall – es stimmte oder aber vielleicht nicht
Was wiederum eine maßlose Übertreibung in die Welt setzt.

6

War is also an attempt to create a new experience
That without experience brought to an end the night darkly

Bidden: this is also an attempt to form words, where
Words without roots, stump and stem wiped out, yet

Not where words crossover placed squealed serene out
Do the forests rest now and then the stubble fields and

Discretion made flesh merely the attempt to master
Without impediments, presented in the temple

Cleared out dreamed away out of the game: here are only
The wild cards, disastrous innocent they know nothing

Supposing that – it were true or rather perhaps not
Which again puts an excessive exaggeration into the world.

7

Und dann standen wir im brutalen Licht wie ein Mann
Wir waren wohlgenährt, ausgebildet in der Kunst, kurzen

Prozeß zu machen, was nicht hieß: Den Kopf riskieren
Einen Kopf kürzer, Licht in einem Kuppelzelt angeknipst

Punktueller Krieg hieß die Phantasie vom schnellen Sieg
Wo wir waren, war Wirklichkeit, wir rückten vor und vor

Schlugen Akazienstämme zur Tarnung. Jeder überwundene
Widerstand regte uns auf, Verheißung ist ein Textkonvoi

Und der befohlene Optimismus stellt an den Nachschub
Außergewöhnliche Anforderungen, sich einen zermürbten

Gegner auszumalen war Pflicht, für uns dachten Großschädel
(Pferde), manchem Pferd tut Lehm, Wasser, eine Nebelwand wohl.

7

And then we stood in the cruel light like men
We were well fed, accomplished in the art of giving

Short shrift, which did not mean: risking one's head
A head shorter, light switched on in the domed tent

Selective war meant the illusion of quick victory
Where we were, was reality, we advanced further and further

Pounded acacia trunks into camouflage. Each resistance
We crushed excited us, promise is a text convoy

And the commanded optimism places extraordinary
Demands on the reserves, to envision a demoralized

Enemy was obligatory, for us great skulls thought
(Horses), many a horse thrives on loam, water, a fog wall.

8

Keine Zeit auszuhalten ohne Rückhalt, um Mehl zu bitten
Weil das Haus immer noch dasselbe, nur eine Ecke weg

Und ein Kalenderblatt unbeschadet an der getünchten Wand
Uhr war stehengeblieben und schaut die rollenden Panzer an

Rausgezerrt wie chiffrierte Bilder, Splittersatz und Abersatz
Verlangen nach Überschaubarkeit, Landkartenverhältnisse

So weitermachen, als würde etwas durch uns selbst geschehen
Lösten sich Blumen von blassem Schaum in den Mundwinkeln

Pioniere im Flußwasser gespiegelt, Betonbrückengeländer
Weggesprengt, hangelten ungesichert an der langen Leine

Der Angst vor dem Tod, Holperstraßen und weicher Teer
Blanke Verfehlung mit Menschenfeuer und Schubkraft

                                        Befehlsgemäß

8

No time to hold out without support to request flour
Because the house still the same, only a corner gone

And a calendar page unscathed on the whitewashed wall
Clock stood still and watching the rolling tanks

Yanked out like encoded pictures, splinter- and however-phrases
Longing for straightforwardness, cartographic relationships

Continuing thus, as if something would happen by ourselves
Did flowers dissolve from the pale foam in the corners of our mouths

Pioneers reflected in the river water, concrete balustrades
Blown away, clinging unsecured to the long line

Of the fear of death, bumpy streets and soft tar
Clear lapse with human fire and shearing force

As ordered

9

Die Saat ging umstandslos auf, eine vertikale Bewegung
Grün schimmernd, vielleicht ist „Untotsein" das richtige Wort

Um Beschmutzung vorzubeugen, das ganze Dorf paßte
Nicht in die Kirche, die im Dorf gelassen aufgelassen brannte

Und die Karre im Dreck, kein Hahn kräht (geschlachtet)
Wie Schädel, Gebein, Trümmer in Plastiksäcken geborgen

Der vorgeschriebene Vorgang in nackten Tatsachen, gib uns
Ernüchterung in der Gluthitze, richtet sich nach der Situation

Wir zogen daraus die Inkonsequenz, dem Feueraugenschein
Nach nicht zu trauen, Rauchsäule stieg auf, Ruß, Rauchopfer

Auf der Bildfläche die vorgeschriebene Wartezeit einhalten
Bevor wir los: Staunen, wie eine Kirche brennt, Schreiende

Darin

9

The seed bore fruit uneventfully, a vertical motion
Lustrous green, perhaps "being undead" is the right word

In order to prevent contamination, the entire village did not
Fit into the church, which left in the village left open burned

And the cart in the dirt, no rooster crows (slaughtered)
Like skulls, bone, debris salvaged in plastic bags

The prescribed procedure in hard facts, disillusion us
In the blazing heat, this suits the situation

From which we drew the contradiction not to trust according to
The appearance of fire, column of smoke arose, soot, smoke offerings

On the picture screen observing the prescribed waiting period
Before we go: amazement, how a church burns, people screaming

                                                              Inside

10

Mit gänzlich untauglichen Mitteln, mit Schaufeln, Hacken
Bloßen Händen im Sand: ein stimmloser Raum, in den

Die Befreier vordringen, Okkupation der Sprache, Uniform=
Teile. Übermalung, Spuren mit untauglichen Händen beseitigt

Benennen, das magischen Charakter hat. Doch ist die Macht
Allerdings nicht in der Lage – Schnitt („infiziert sich selbst")

Benennen, das willenlos hüllenlos: Sind die Reifen neu auf=
Gezogen mit Händen zu greifen, knirscht etwas? Fuselbilder

Begegnungen in den ausgeräumten Wölbungen der Macht
Hitze steht darin, auch Geruch von verbranntem Gummi

Schüttere Zedern am Rand, unpassierbar die Furt, Sicherheits=
Abstand: minimal. Der Schatten des Objekts legt sich aufs Ich.

10

With entirely unfit means, with shovels, hoes
Bare hands in the sand: a voiceless room in which

The liberators advance, occupation of the language, uniform
Parts. New paint, traces abolished by unfit hands

Naming that has magical character. Yet power is
Certainly not in a position – cut ("infects itself")

Naming that without will, without cover: have the tires recently been
Mounted to grasp by hand, is something grinding? Fusel pictures

Encounters in the cleared-out curvatures of power
Heat dwells within, also smell of burned rubber

Sparse cedars at the edge, the ford impassable, safe
Distance: minimal. The shadow of the object lies upon the ego.

11

Bis wir so leise sprachen, daß man neben unseren Worten
Auch unsere Stimmen hörte. Aber die kehllauten Stimmen

Stören nicht, haltlos im Kopf, Stresscode, taubengurrend oder
Trällernd im Einverständnis mit den Phonemen, Phänomenen

Faktisch aus dem Verkehr gezogen, süß kaugummiverklebt
Der müde Mund eine lautlos geschlossene Veranstaltung

Oder Paketband, daß Schreie und Nichtschreie kriegstauglich
Wären, kämen aus dem geschlossenen Mund, der dann aber

Endgültig (Gedächtnisspeicher für die Szene des Angriffs)
Bis wir so leise sprachen, schacherten, Sonne stand glorios

Heller die Stimmen wie Täuschung, Erleuchtung und Augen
Am Visier, die Einschleusung von Wirklichkeit ist ein Vorrecht.

11

Until we spoke so quietly that besides our words
One also heard our voices. But the guttural voices

Do not disturb, unstable in the head, stress code, doves cooing or
Warbling in agreement with the phonemes, phenomena

Virtually phased out, sweetly stuck like chewing gum
The tired mouth a silently restricted performance

Or package cord, that screams and non-screams would be fit
For war, would come from the closed mouth which then however

Conclusively (memory storage for the scene of the attack)
Until we spoke so quietly, bartered, sun stood glorious

The voices clearer like illusion, enlightenment and eyes
On the sight, the infiltration of reality is a privilege.

12

Ja, diese Befangenheit, Beklommenheit, Hut ab, Helm ab
Shut up das Magazin leergeballert: ein virtuelles Stöhnen

Oder Tonspur, kein Mensch, kein Kind, keinen *Tort* angetan
Fünfmal hat man dir schon nach dem Leben getrachtet (vergeblich)

Das im Maschinentakt weiterpochte, als spielten wir auf Zeit
Die dann schon vergangen war beim vorschnellen Beginnen

Eine Ernüchterung, die stattfand, nicht stattgegeben, Doppel=
Deutigkeit, mit der Wucht eines Tupfers und dann der Aufprall

Der in der Luft blieb, stilles Staunen und ekstatisches Jubeln
(„Noch nicht, diesmal noch nicht, der nächste Zug bricht durch.")

Du stehst auf wie gänzlich unbesiegbar, eine Überlegenheit
Des blanken Zufalls. Man befiehlt oder bittet doch nicht ständig.

12

Yes, this awkwardness, anguish, hat off, helmet off
Shut up the magazine shot empty: a virtual moaning

Or sound track, no person, no child, no tort forced
Five times already they have sought your life (in vain)

That beats on in machine pulse, as if we were playing for time
Which had already run out at the overhasty beginning

A disenchantment that occurred, not granted, double
Entendre, with the force of one dabbing, and then the impact

That remained in the air, silent amazement and ecstatic jubilation
("Not yet, this time not yet, the next platoon will break through.")

You stand up completely invincible, a transcendence
Of pure coincidence. They will not always command or request.

III

Faszination

Blockbuster Byron

III

Fascination

Blockbuster Byron

1

Alles ist groß, alles soll groß sein. Größer als. Am Größten.
(Was nicht groß ist, wird übersehen.) Übertrieben. Alles im
Als Ob. Und nicht geringer. Darüber muß gegangen werden
Mit schnellem Schritt und hocherhobenen Hauptes und Mutes.
Über das Heldische. Ein erhabener Gegenstand in eigener Person.
Den Pferdeleib besteigen, Anpassung des Körpers an den Pferdeleib
Regentschaft über den Hyper-Leib, den Pferd und Reiter bilden.
Druck ausüben, Druck verteilen, die Schenkel denken. Später
Die Kutsche besteigen, den Schlag schließen, die Zügel anziehen
Und dann schießen lassen. Er hat im festen Griff, was er tut
Er hat das englischste England im Griff, Liebling der Aristokratie
Die Ladies ihm zu Füßen. Einen Fuß zieht er nach, Künstlerpech.

1

All is great, all should be great. Greater than. The greatest.
(What is not great will be overlooked.) Exaggerated. All things
As If. And not less. One must go beyond that
With a swift pace and head and spirits held high.
Beyond the heroic. A sublime purpose in one's own person.
Mounting the steed, alignment of the body to the steed
Regency over the hyper-body, which horse and rider form.
Exerting pressure, dispersing pressure, thinking the thighs. Later
Mounting the coach, felling the blow, tightening the reins
And then beginning to shoot. He firmly masters what he does
He masters the most English England, darling of the aristocracy
The ladies at his feet. One foot he drags along, artist's misfortune.

2

Sehr spitz die Verse, die er schreibt, und ganz England lacht.
Man schreibt nicht für England, nicht für die Ladies, Veilchen
Schnupftabakdosen, *having no teachers*, schreibt für die Toten, die
Geschrieben haben, bevor man schrieb, die Toten in den Gräbern
Und in der Bibliothek: Lederrücken und Staub, Wörterlisten, Verse
A blending of all beauties. Ye stars, which are the poetry of heaven!
Die Ladies proben das Naserümpfen. So war das nicht gedacht
Ausgemacht. Spielverderber, hinterläßt er Scherben, nach ihm
Die Sintflut. Andere schlagen Schlachten, gründen Städte oder –
Er schreibt Verse, als gründe er Aktiengesellschaften, ein Bergwerk
Eisenbahnlinien, eine Welt in Worten, angerichtet auf dem Silbertablett:
Das zur Verfügung Stehende, das Mach- und Denkbare (in seinem Hirn).

2

Very keen, the verses that he writes, and all of England laughs.
One does not write for England, not for the ladies, violets
Snuff boxes, having no teachers, writes for the dead, who
Have written before he wrote, the dead in their graves
And in the library: leatherbacks and dust, word lists, verses
A blending of all beauties. Ye stars, which are the poetry of heaven!
The ladies practice turning up their noses. It was not meant that way
Agreed. Spoil sport, he leaves behind shards, after him
The deluge. Others fight battles, found cities or –
He writes verse, as if he were founding corporations, a mine
Railway lines, a world in words, arranged on a silver platter:
Whatever is available, the doable and imaginable (in his brain).

3

Er erwachte eines Morgens und fand, daß er ein berühmter Mann sei.
Niemand widersprach, und er gab sich selbst recht. Wie das Wort
Ihm schmeichelte, wie das Wort entschlief, als jene Welt erwachte
Welt aus Gewißheit, Vogelnestern, dämonischem Knistern. Kraft
Zur Erfindung seiner selbst auf dem Feld einer unbezwingbaren Idee
Vogelflug über den Weiden, die Gatter geöffnet bis zum Gehölz.
Im Hohen Haus zu sitzen von hoher Geburt, im Sattel sitzen, schwitzen
Und geritten, gerissen zu werden von der Lust zu reiten, streiten ohne
Unterlaß. Die Signale von den Gefährdungen des Lebens mißachten
Entschlossenheit kalt zum Ausdruck bringen, ohne den Schlüssel
Abrakadabra – ohne den Schlüssel preiszugeben – letztlich ohne
Eine einzige Öffnung. Aber die Leidenschaft eine Erfindung.

3

He awoke one morning and found that he was a famous man.
No one disagreed, and he proved himself right. Just as the word
Flattered him, as the word fell asleep, when that world awoke
World of certainty, bird's-nests, demonic crackling. Strength
For the invention of himself in the field of an indomitable idea
Bird flight over the meadows, the gates opened, up to the thicket.
To sit in the Upper House by high birth, sitting in the saddle, sweating
And to be ridden, to be rent by the desire to ride, fighting without
Ceasing. Disregarding the signals of the endangering of life
Coldly giving expression to determination, without the code
Abracadabra – without divulging the code – ultimately without
A single opening. Nevertheless the passion an invention.

4

Mit starken Gesten austeilend, vorauseilend, ein Schuß, ein Genuß
Man muß die Schnepfe im Flug vom flanellgrauen Himmel holen
Der Hund apportiert, alles gelingt, alles machtvoll, sich mächtig
Hinunterneigend, der nachschleifende Fuß, der demütige Gruß
Man muß sich zu den Gegenständen wenden, sich ihnen zeigen
Damit sie sich entfalten. Alle Zuckungen enden in Versen, also
Hochgemut aufgesteilt, was haben Sie für schöne Pistolen, *dear*?
Der Dichter schont die Sprache so wenig wie die Menschen. Betreibt
Das Schießen durchaus systematisch. Der Blick muß schweifen, reifen
Damit man ihn nicht sieht. *This time we should return to plain
Narration*, wir wenden uns dem Dunklen zu, dem Wilden, Pockigen
„Madame, ich bedaure sehr die Störung Ihrer Nachmittagsruhe."

4

Dispensing, anticipating with strong gestures, a shot, a joy
One must fetch the snipe in flight from the flannel-gray sky
The dog retrieves, all goes well, all powerful, all mighty
Leaning down, the foot dragging behind, the humble hello
One must devote oneself to objects, appear to them
So that they unfold. All convulsions end in verses, therefore
High spirits steepened, what lovely pistols have you, dear?
The poet spares language as little as he does people. Conducts
The shooting entirely methodically. The gaze must roam, ripen
So that it is not seen. This time we should return to plain
Narration, we turn towards the darkness, the wild, pockmarked
"Madam, I sincerely regret disrupting your afternoon nap."

5

Als Student in Cambridge übt er die Hand. Die Hand wird ruhig
Verliert das Zittern. Er schießt auf Marder, die sich ihm entziehn
Ein falscher Weg: Er schießt auf Hühner, schießt den Hühnern
Die Köpfe vom Hals. Die Hühner werden zum Dinner serviert.
Nehmet und esset, dies ist mein Fleisch, dies ist die Hühnersuppe
Mit fetten Augen und Karotten. Er schießt einer Dame ein Loch
In den Hut, aber die Dame ist zu vornehm, um sich zu beklagen
Entfesselt sich, der nie gefesselt war. Prometheus *revisited*
Betreibt das Schießen halbwegs systematisch, will es beherrschen
Das Töten beherrschen, nicht nur im Hühnerstall, überall. Versucht
Sich Wichtigkeit zu geben in der Form des blind Schuldigen oder
Verfluchten, schwarze schwerflüssige Tinte der Dämonie, Dynastie.

5

As a student at Cambridge he trains his hand. It becomes steady
Stops trembling. He shoots at martens, which elude him
The wrong path: He shoots at chickens, shoots the heads of the
Chickens off their necks. The chickens are served for supper.
Take and eat, this is my body, this is the chicken soup
With drops of grease and carrots. He shoots a hole in the hat
Of a lady, but the lady is too proper to lodge a complaint
Unleashes himself, he who was never bound. Prometheus revisited
Conducts the shooting halfway methodically, wants to control it
To control the killing, not only in the chicken coop, everywhere. Tries
To lend himself importance by being blindly guilty or
Cursed, black viscous ink of demonical possession, dynasty.

6

Haschisch, Huren, Homosexualität und eine Hochzeitsnacht
Das sich eisig kalt gewaschen hat. Eine ahnungslose junge Frau
Dann weiß sie. (Und will nicht wissen warum.) „Nun ist es
Zu spät", kommentiert der Gatte das ihr anvertraute Unglück.
Und er hat wieder recht. Es war schön, in der einen Frau zu sein
Und es war schön, nicht in der Frau zu sein. Im Gebüsch. Im Moor.
Zu Pferde. Im Wasser. Überall Glück, nimmermüdes Verlangen.
Es war schön, in der Schwester zu sein. Das hättest du nicht
Gedacht, daß du beginnen würdest in hochgespannter Zeit
Beginnen die lange Schlängellinie des heroischen Lebens
Und Schreibens, etwas zerspringt, erst eines, dann das andere
In kühler Explosion oder beidhändig schlecht ausgefochten.

6

Hashish, whores, homosexuality and a honeymoon night
That washed up ice cold. An unsuspecting young woman
Then she knows. (And does not want to know why.) "Now it is
Too late," the bridegroom comments on her confided misfortune.
And he is right again. It was nice to be in the one woman
And it was nice not to be in the woman. In the shrubs. In the swamp.
On a horse. In the water. Everywhere bliss, never-tiring desire.
It was nice to be in the sister. This you would not have
Thought, that you would begin in a period of high tension
Begin the long meandering line of the heroic life
And of writing, something shatters, first one, then the other
In cool explosion or ambidextrously, poorly fought out.

7

Bereit, den poetischen Gesetzgeber der Welt zu mimen, die sich
Das gern gefallen läßt. Bürgert sich selber aus, verkauft Grund
Und Boden, will bodenlos sein, nie mehr ein geordnetes Haus
Gemietete *palazzi, casini,* düstre Zimmer in feuchtkalten *alberghi*
Um die eine Geliebte zu empfangen, die andere zu demissionieren
Händel, Briefschaften, Manuskripte, die venezianischen Stiefel
Drücken, ein ruinierter Dandy im Exil, Provokateur, Marodeur
In fremden Leben, Ehen, Betten, mit vierzehn Dienstboten in Venedig
Mit Hunden, einem Affen, Katzen, Papageien, dem Bastardkind
Wie er es nennt. Viel Holz, viel Ehr, viel Wirbel und dann Rückzug
Zu Papier und Tinte, zu Zeilenbrüchen, polemischen Abstürzen
Es ist besser, etwas zu tun, als nichts zu tun. Invasion der Wörter.

7

Prepared to mimic the poetic legislator of the world that gladly
Puts up with that. Expatriates himself, sells property and
Land, wants to be unbound, never again an orderly house
Rented *palazzi*, *casini*, dreary rooms in clammy *alberghi*
In order to receive one mistress, to renounce the other one
Commerce, correspondence, manuscripts, the Venetian boots
Pinching, a ruined dandy in exile, agitator, marauder
In foreign lives, marriages, beds, with fourteen servants in Venice
With dogs, a monkey, cats, parrots, the bastard child as he calls it.
A lot of baggage, of honor, of fuss and then retreat
To paper and ink, to line breaks, polemical crashes
It is better to do something than nothing. Invasion of words.

8

„Was bedeutet dieses merkwürdige Wort radikal, das es
In meiner Jugend nicht gegeben hat?" Auftrumpfen, Aushöhlen
Wurzellos sich selbst erfinden unter der Draperie, Mechanik
Der Geschichte, der in den Arm gefallen, rasierte Briefstellen
Ausradierte Individuen, Intrigen, Massaker in den oberen Rängen
Geschichte ist ein Puzzle, in dem jeweils ein Stück fehlt. Phantasien
Sind Kostümproben, mein einziger Feind: die profunde Langeweile.
Oder habe ich etwas falsch verstanden? Ich erinnere einen Zeitvertreib
Das Kind stach Nadeln in die dicklichen Arme seiner Mutter, die
Wehrte sich nicht, haltlose Zeit, stures Klammern an die Sicherheit
Eines ererbten Titels; obgleich es an Talent und Energie nicht mangelt
Um zu Ruhm zu kommen. Dichten Aktienbesitzer, Kohlebarone? Nicht?

8

"What does this curious word radical mean which
Was unknown in my youth?" Exulting, excavating
Rootlessly inventing himself under the drapery, mechanics
Of history that fell into his arms, cut-out letter passages
Rubbed-out individuals, intrigues, massacres in the upper echelons
History is a jigsaw puzzle which always has a piece missing.
Fantasies are dress rehearsals, my only foe: profound boredom.
Or did I understand something incorrectly? I remember a pastime
The child stuck needles in the pudgy arms of his mother, who
Did not defend herself, unstable time, stubbornly clinging to the security
Of an inherited title; although there is no lack of talent and energy
To achieve fame. Do shareholders, coal barons write poetry? No?

9

Neunzehn Abgeordnete begehen Selbstmord in England, dem Wahnsinn
Verfallen zwanzig in einer Generation, blanke Ernüchterung, haltlose Zeit
Nachnapoleonisch geordnet, kaserniert, vergiftete Ideale kalt gemacht
Freiheit ein angestochener Luftballon in einem Polizeistaat aufgeflogen
Oder: „Ich bin mir gewiß, daß ich niemals besser geschrieben habe als –
Wenn ihr es nicht merkt, wünsche ich Euch allen einen besseren
Geschmack." Untadelig der seine, die Verse klingen, klingeln, er trotzt
Den päpstlichen Legaten, Spitzel öffnen Briefe, denunzieren, intrigieren
Der Lido leckt den Sand, er leckt sich seine Wunden, geschlagen
Nicht, Zeuge des Abschlagens von drei Männerköpfen in Italien
Und einer Kindesvorhaut. An der Kutsche baumelt ein Käfig mit Gänsen
So will er die Österreicher vertreiben, verhöhnt den päpstlichen Legaten.

9

Nineteen representatives commit suicide in England, twenty
In a generation go insane, sheer disenchantment, unstable time
Post-napoleonically arranged, barracked, poisoned ideals turned cold
Freedom a punctured balloon released in a police state
Or: "I am certain that I have never written better than –
If you do not notice it, I wish you all a better sense of
Taste." His own irreproachable, the verses sound, ring, he defies
The papal legates, informants open letters, denunciate, machinate
The lido licks the sand, he licks his wounds, not beaten
Witness to the cutting off of three human heads in Italy
And a child's foreskin. On the coach dangles a cage with geese
Thus he wants to drive out the Austrians, derides the papal legates.

10

Das anvertraute Gut, das heiße Blut, die Ländereien, Vogelherde.
Der Rebell rebelliert, zu leise, zu konventionell. Schöne Wörter
Umschatten ihn. Sich hinunterneigend, das Boot besteigend, und wo
Ein Wille ist, ist später uferloses Gestrüpp. Sind Ziegenpfade, Hitze
Staub zu überwinden, die Waffen rostig wie Worte, überflüssig.
Warum lädt sich einer eine Welt auf, die nicht seine ist? Fraglich
Für wen? Warum verläßt einer eine Welt, die sich ihm schmiegte
In die weiche Hand, in sein angeborenes Land, vergeben die Schande
Der Geschwisterliebe: *The whole man must move at once.* Hofmannsthal
Zitiert Byron, die Achmatowa zitiert, und die Bewegung zittert noch
In der heißen Luft. Signale der Gefährdung des Lebens mißachten
Sich selbst achten, überschätzen, Pfeffer streuen, daß jemand niest.

10

The entrusted belongings, blood unsated, manors, fowling-floors.
The rebel rebels, too quietly, too conventionally. Nice words
Shade him. Leaning down, climbing into the boat, and where
There's a will, there is boundless undergrowth. Can goat paths,
Heat, dust be overcome, weapons rusty as words, superfluous.
Why does one take on a world that is not one's own? Questionable
For whom? Why does one leave a world that was eating
From one's hand, in one's native country, forgiven the disgrace
Of sibling incest: The whole man must move at once. Hofmannsthal
Quotes Byron, Akhmatova quotes, and the movement still trembles
In the hot air. Disregarding the signals of endangering life
Attending to oneself, overestimating, sprinkling pepper so someone sneezes.

11

Emissär der Philhellenischen Gesellschaft London *in extremis*
Plötzlich durch den Süden irrend, der fremder als jeder Norden
Engagement, Europaschwärmerei, Exzentrik von hohen Gnaden
Schwermut und Schminke, Exzesse und Edelmut, Verlangen
Im Reinzustand, der so rein ist wie ein Gepansche in Kellern.
Ein Spielrausch *in extremis* auf Serie gesetzt, was langweilt.
Weder Schreie noch Trümmer, die Logistik langwierig. *Why?*
Kein Handumdrehn fürs Dichten, alles ist schwer und leicht zugleich
Anders als in Deutschland, in dem immer die Gänse watscheln
Auf großen Füßen ohne Grüße an jemanden in der Welt. Man bleibt
Für sich oder kauft sich ein Stück Welt und treibt die Kosten hoch
Ehe man sich's versieht. *(Why do they hate us? Why do they spit?)*

11

Emissary of the Philhellenic Society of London *in extremis*
Suddenly erring through the South, more foreign than any North
Dedication, European fanaticism, eccentricity of high mercies
Melancholy and make-up, excesses and generosity, desire
In pure condition, as pure as an adulteration in cellars.
A playing frenzy *in extremis* set in a series, which is dull.
Neither screams nor debris, logistics wearisome. Why?
No snap of the fingers to write poetry, all is at once difficult and easy
Different than in Germany, where the geese always waddle
On big feet without greeting anybody in the world. One keeps
To oneself or buys oneself a piece of the world and drives the prices up
Before one knows it. (Why do they hate us? Why do they spit?)

12

Don Juan, der siebzehnte Gesang: eine Wunde, in der Blut pocht
Der Regen poltert an das Zeltdach, und Wege versinken im Lehm
Noch einmal Lepanto, noch einmal haushoch über die Osmanen siegen.
Kriege sind schöngeredet, während die rostigen Pistolen im Regen
Klemmen, Söldner, die fordern, fördern. Ein Hauen und Stechen
Diplomatie ist Seife und Taktieren, im Morast versinkt die Kampfmoral
Erpresser, Schwindler, Großsprecher: Sie wollen Geld, Hilfe, einen Rang
Oder himmelblaue Uniformhosen, wie der Griechenknabe, der ihm dient.
„Ich stimme Forderungen zu, die mich überfordern." Unendlich müde
Macht der Kampf, der nicht gekämpft, nicht zu gewinnen, ein Melodram
Nur nicht den Kopf verlieren, das Fieber steigt, in Schüttelfrösten frieren.
Der schmale Türkenmond steht da in fremder Sprache, fremdem Land.

12

Don Juan, the seventeenth canto: a wound in which blood throbs
The rain blusters on the tent roof, and paths sink away into the loam
Again Lepanto, again winning enormously over the Ottomans.
Wars are rhetoricized, while the rusty pistols jam in the rain
Mercenaries, who demand, support. Hewing and stabbing
Diplomacy is soap and plotting, in the quagmire morale sinks
Blackmailers, swindlers, braggarts: They want money, help, a rank
Or sky-blue uniform pants, like the Greek lad who serves him.
"I agree to demands that ask too much of me." Ceaselessly tired
By the battle not fought, not to be won, a melodrama
Just not losing one's head, the fever rises, freezing with chills.
The slender Turkish moon hangs there in foreign tongue, foreign land.

IV

Operation

Klopfzeichen

Wer sich vor dem Tode fürchtet, tut wohl am besten sich gleich tot zu schießen, denn diese Furcht quält ihn sonst bei jeder Veranlassung täglich, und setzt ihn in Gefahr, Niederträchtigkeiten und Schurkereien zu begehen.

Johann Gottfried Seume, Apokryphen

IV

Operation

Knocking

Whoever is afraid of death should probably just shoot himself right away because this fear will otherwise torture him daily on every occasion and place him in danger of committing vile acts and villainies.

Johann Gottfried Seume, Apocrypha

1

Was wir sahen, sahen wir nicht wirklich: Verbluten.
Sahen ein Sickern, eine Färbung, wie Laub sich färbt

(Nur rascher) wir sahen das Staunen, ein Tasten nach
Feuchtigkeit, die Blut war. Wenn Sehen Geschehen ist

Geschah uns etwas. Wir sahen unsere Helme rutschen über
Die Schulter hinweg, wir sahen, wie Zinn schmilzt, tropfend

Stehen blieb ein Teil, war's ein Pfahl, im Feuer verglüht
Wie jemand hinstürzt, sahen wir tagtäglich, noch lebendig

Sahen das Weiße in den Augen nicht hinter Schutzbrillen
Sahen einen Bogen fliegen und eine Hand durchbohren

Beinah einer getötet. Wir sahen den Schrei aus dem Mund
Gurgeln, sahen auf Kartenblättern saubere Geraden. Schnitt.

1

What we saw we didn't really see: bleeding to death.
Saw an oozing, a coloration, like leaves turning color

(Only more rapidly) we saw amazement, groping for
Moisture that was blood. Whenever seeing happened

Something happened to us. We saw our helmets slip
Down over our shoulders, we saw how tin melts, dripping

A part stood still, was it a pole, smoldering in the fire
Like someone topples over, we saw day after day, still alive

Saw the whites of their eyes not behind safety glasses
Saw an arrow flying and then piercing a hand

One nearly killed. We saw the scream from his mouth
Gurgling, saw clean straight lines on map pages. Cut.

2

Die dann geschleppt und vergraben, namenlos verscharrt
Starre, Starre, Totenstarre, die Muskeln und Gelenk ergreift

So daß kein Stiefel die lastende Stille zwischen Blech
Und Sandkörnern tritt. Doch die Sohlen immer marsch=

Bereit Augen und Mund, das Lochmuster der Einschüsse
Wohin mit den Augen, woher gewendet der Blick (komm mit!)

Gestochen scharfe Bilder gehen über die Hügelketten ins Auge
Gesplitterte Bäume knirschen im Wind, der Wolken mitbringt

Eingenähte Amulette, Milchzähne und so unter Schutz=
Westen aufgehobene Dinge: Knochen und Photographien

Zersetzungsgeschichte eines Angriffs durch Windbruch
Knirscht zwischen den Zähnen „niemand war gefaßt auf"

2

Those then hauled away and buried, namelessly in shallow graves
With dirt, rigor, rigor, rigor mortis gripping muscles and joints

So that no boot treads the oppressive silence between tin
And grains of sand. Nonetheless the soles always ready to

Move eyes and mouth, the perforated pattern of bullet holes
Where to look, whence the gaze turned (come along!)

Needle-sharp pictures go over the range of hills to the eyes
Slivered trees rustle in the wind, bringing clouds along

Amulets sewn in, baby teeth and such beneath safety
Vests preserved things: bones and photographs

Decomposition history of an attack by windfall
Gnashes between the teeth "no one bargained for"

3

Verteilt den Tod so lang, daß er dem unebenen Leben ähnelte
Verteilt den Tod ins Flächige, den Raum, den er besetzt

In einer Welt aus Stein und Schotter versteinern Perspektiven
Ist jede Aussage anfechtbar, und wer sie in den Mund nimmt

Dem erstirbt sie. Wer einmal, zweimal die Lippe blutig gebissen
Wer sich den Wörtern ergeben hat, die kommen und gehen

Nicht bleiben, aufplatzen („als hätten sie keine Bedeutung gehabt")
Wer eine ganze Nacht hellhörig: immer wieder Schneegesträuch

Das die Hände ritzt, im Frühjahr Himmelskeime ausgelegt
Und Stein für Stein, die dann ins Rollen kamen an blassen

Hängen – du arbeitest an etwas mit, das du nicht verstehst
Trägst die Steine, die zerpulvern, und du bist nicht wortlos.

3

Disperse death for so long that it begins to resemble uneven life
Disperse death into the expanse, the space that it occupies

In a world of stone and rubble perspectives turn to stone
Is every statement debatable, and whoever gives it voice

To him it fades away. Whoever once, twice bit his lips bloody
Whoever has surrendered himself to words which come and go

Not remaining, bursting ("as if they had had no meaning")
Whoever clairaudient for an entire night: snow shrubs again and again

Which scratch the hands, in springtime heaven seeds planted
And stone for stone which began to roll on pale slopes –

You are collaborating on something you do not understand
Carrying the stones that are pulverized and you are not wordless.

4

Uns waren die Hände gebunden, nicht aber die Augen
Und die Pupillen, atropingeweitet starr gegen das Licht

Gerichtet, also durchlässig für Morgenkälte, Erstgeburten
Zeltlager ohne Isoliermatten, so warteten wir, was geschähe

Letztendlich auf uns selbst, diese stumpfen Ausflüchte, die
Nichts spüren wollten außer dem angetanen Kalkül, *jieperten*

(Wie der Jäger sagt) nach weitreichender Erfahrung, in der
Alles einen Wert hat, „folglich" belohnt werden will. Horchten

Auf den Ton des Tages, Tagesverfassung gereizt: Geräusche
Himmelsöffnungen oder eine Staubwolke, Eselsprozession

Die mit rebellischer Stirn das Dornengesträuch streifte
So daß die Augen, Flackersterne, sich schon entschieden

4

Our hands were bound, however not our eyes
And the pupils, atropine-dilated numbly focused

On the light, thus permeable to the morning cold, first births
Tent camps without isolation mats, we waited like this, what

Would happen, ultimately for ourselves, these dull evasions which
Didn't want to feel anything except the apt calculations, craved

(Like the hunter says) wide-ranging experience, in which
All has a value, wants to be rewarded "accordingly." Harkened

To the tone of the day, mood of the day irritable: sounds
Ports of heaven or a cloud of dust, procession of donkeys

Which touched the thorn bushes with rebellious brow
So that the eyes, flickering stars, had already decided

5

Ein Schuldgefühl, das seine Schuld erst noch finden muß
Das sich schamhaft verbirgt, schutzsuchend im Kugel=

Sicheren („wenn man dich nicht füsiliert"), die Aussicht
Auf den geordneten Lazarettplatz blendend und beruhigend

„Robert, der Riese, Artillerist, wird bei Schießereien so kalt
Und erregt, daß er meine Hand nimmt, sich aufs Herz legt

Und festpreßt: Fürchtest du dich gar nicht? Als ich sagte: Nein.
Fürchte mich überhaupt nie, seufzt er tief auf: Das ist gut, das

Tut mir so wohl." Überdies wird genügend Branntwein gereicht
Erinnerung wie Tiere, die blökend ihre Herde verloren und

Hilflos waren. Wild war auf Straßen in der Nacht geblendet
Im Graben verendet, so war das Fleisch knochenmühlenreif.

5

Feelings of guilt that must still find their reason
Bashfully hiding, seeking shelter in something bullet –

Proof ("if they don't arm you with a fusel"), the view
Of the orderly field hospital brilliant and soothing

"Robert, the giant, artilleryman, gets so cold and excited
During the shooting he takes my hand, places it on his heart

And presses it tightly: Aren't you at all afraid? When I said: No.
Actually not ever afraid, he heaves a sigh: That is good, that

Does me such good." Moreover plenty of brandy is passed around
Memory like animals who, bleating, lost their flock and

Were helpless. Deer were blinded on streets at night dying
In the trenches so the meat was ready for the bone crusher.

6

Kleine Verschläge und Höhlen, jeweils zu dreien und vieren
In denen wir horchten und horchten in fremde Leben hinein

Roberts eisige Hand Klammergriff, unschuldiges Plappern
Mit Akazienstämmchen und Laub sind wir perfekt getarnt

Habe ich, obwohl noch nie in einer Schlacht, eine eigentümliche
Leere gespürt, als fehlte etwas, was hart macht, was Angst ist

Robert, der furchtsame Artillerist, Körper wie ein Bär und
Sommersprossiges Kindergemüt, will mir ein Photo zeigen

Frau im Geblümten, mit einer Handtasche vor dem Busen
Bewehrt, er weiß nicht, wo sie ist. Wälzt sich halbwach

Verdreht im Fell und haarverwüstet, die Läufe geknickt
Während die Nacht tiefer und tiefer in den Körper sinkt.

6

Small shelters and caves, each with groups of three and four
In which we harkened and harkened into foreign lives

Robert's icy hand clamping grip, innocent chattering
With acacia logs and foliage we are perfectly disguised

I have, though never yet in battle, sensed a peculiar void,
As if something were missing that toughens, that is fear

Robert, the fearful artilleryman, body like a bear and
Freckled child's mind, wants to show me a photo

Woman in a flowered dress, armed with a handbag in front of
Her bosom, he doesn't know where she is. Wallows half-awake

Twisted in fur and hair ravaged, muzzles cocked
While the night sinks deeper and deeper into the body.

7

Untaugliche Hände, untaugliche Münder, in Sprache getaucht
Kopfunter getaucht in Schüsseln, Eimer, Klosetts untragbar

Untauglich gewässert, es war die erste Übung, die gründlich
Mißlang. Leugnung war nicht vorgesehen, vorgestern noch

Leuchtende Parolen, wir werden, uns gehört, Sonnengötter
In rollenden Kolonnen, einzelne stürzen, was ist Sieg, wenn

Der Widerstand bricht im Genick, Widerstand, Widerhall
Hast, ein Handel mit Worten, Zitaten, gefälschten Zeugnissen

Aufbruch auch. Die *Pick-ups* in der Gluthitze gepackt, geparkt
Schüttellähmung der Gefühle, strophisch gefiltertes Wasser ebbt

Wie träge Vögel an Wasserstellen, wehrhafte Pumpstationen
Und kein Mensch weit und breit. Wie Augen, die geblendet.

7

Unfit hands, unfit mouths, immersed in language
Immersed head down in basins, pails, latrines unbearable

Unfit rinsing, it was the first attempt which thoroughly
Failed. Denial was not intended, even the day before yesterday

Glaring slogans, we become, we possess, gods of the sun
In rolling convoys, individuals fall, what is victory if

The resistance breaks its neck, resistance, repercussion
Haste, trading in words, references, false testimony

Departure also. The pick-ups packed, parked in the scorching heat
Shaking palsy of feelings, strophically filtered water ebbs

Like sluggish birds at watering holes, well-fortified pumping stations
And no human being far and wide. Like eyes that are blinded.

8

Man muß sich selbst überlisten, um eilig einen Rückzugsraum
Zu durchmessen, illegal aufgehalten unter Aprikosenbäumen

Vor sich selbst versteckt, so daß dann die Körper gedengelt
Herumirrten im Freien, das frei nicht, Wasserflaschen und Deck=

Betten, Dosen mit *Corned Beef*, wo Reisfladen erwartet wurden
Mais & Salznerven, vom Hörensagen bekannt, doch unübersetzbar

Ausgeschüttete Glückshormone und dieses selbstzufriedene Zittern
Wenn alles vorbei, Kontaktaufnahme als elektrische Erregung

Dummköpfe fliegen jetzt herum mit *last-minute*-Buchungen, das Ticket
In der Brusttasche: was kostet die Welt, Geräusche sind Kratertrichter

Umsonst ist nur. Daß unsere Rechnungen nicht aufgehen, wußten
Wir längst und gingen blicklos grollend in ausgehobene Gräben.

8

One must outsmart oneself to swiftly traverse the range
Of a retreat, illegally squatting under apricot trees

Hidden from oneself so that the bodies, thinned, strayed
Into the open that is not open, water bottles and feather –

Beds, cans of corned beef, where rice paddies were expected
Corn & salt nerves, known from hearsay but untranslatable

Released endorphins and this self-satisfied trembling
When everything is over, establishing contacts as electrical charge

Dumb asses now run around with last-minute reservations, the ticket
In their breast pocket: what price the world, sounds are crater funnels

In vain is only. We knew long ago that our bills do not
Add up and went sulking without a glance into dugout trenches.

9

In der Fälligkeit den Zufall entdecken. Der nicht trog.
Und dann gesagt getan und niemals zu lang gezögert

Ein winziges Waldstück, auf dem Reißbrett entworfen
Zittergras, Sternenmoos, bleichdumpfer Morchelgeruch

Im Nebel zu Haus, Archäologie des schallgedämpften Raumes
Der explodiert vor unseren Augen, die wir schließen, Schock

Eines einzelnen Gedankens (Verdichtung?) so einzigartig nicht
Zugleich trog der Eindruck, als wären Unsummen verschoben

„Wenn die Sonne einmal durch den Panzer grauer Wolken
Sticht" – Abwürfe auf uns Maulwürfe, hörten tote Stimmen

Aller Dinge, die wir vernichteten, aus der Welt hebelten also
Ihre Herren zeitweise mit windgedrehten Flügeln gewinkelt

9

Discovering coincidence on the due date. Which did not deceive.
And then no sooner said than done and never hesitating too long

A tiny patch of woods, designed on the drawing table
Quaking-grass, starry moss, pale-dull smell of morels

At home in the fog, archaeology of the sound-insulated room
That explodes in front of our eyes, which we close, shock

Of a single thought (condensation?) not so unique at the same time
The impression deceived, as if enormous sums were laundered

"When the sun first peeks through the armor of gray
Clouds" – launchings falling on us moles, heard dead voices

Of all things we destroyed removed from the world with levers
As their masters squared off at times with wind-blown wings

10

Ich ging trotz des Morastes ein großes Stück spazieren
Noch einmal ein Stück russischer Landschaft, unbetreten

Ich betrat Welt, die nicht in Scherben, und der Schlamm
Zog runter, ich blieb Grasnarbe wie ein Schnupftuch groß

Mein Stab liegt hier, endlich wieder Landschaft, Weg
Führt hinaus ins Sandige, sprach mit einem Zehlendorfer

Dem Urlaub gewährt, den ich ausgeschlagen, nachrückende
Vögel, Elstergezeter, wo bin ich denn, wenn nicht todesnah

Nähe ist ein Mittel gegen Dunkelheit, Ökonomie des Mitleids
Robert so traurig über den Abschied, daß keine Sprache reichte

Ausgeschlagen und eine tote Zeit vertrieben ohne Vorlieben
Oder im Hinterland des Gefühls „als hätt er 1 guten Kameraden"

10

I walked a considerable stretch despite the swamp
Again a stretch of Russian landscape, untrodden

I entered a world, not in shards, and the mud
Drew me down, I remained sod, big as a handkerchief

My stick lies here, finally landscape again, path
Leads out to a sandy area, spoke with a Zehlendorfer

Whose vacation granted, I rejected, advancing birds
Magpie scolding, where am I now, if not near death

Closeness is a remedy for darkness, economy of sympathy
Robert so sad about departing that no words would suffice

Rejected and whiled away lost time without preferences
Or deep down in his feelings "as if he had 1 good buddy"

11

Ganze Wortfelder unter den Reifenspuren in der feuchten Erde
Hörten die Kettenfahrzeuge Kolonnen auf holprigen Straßen

Ahnungen, die im Nachschub stecken, wo sie erwartet, so erhärtet
Schwarze Feuer schwelen im Nebel, Zucken der Bodenwellen

Ballast abwerfen und den versengten Mantel, die Zeit ist Schutz
Wie jedem kleinen Felltier, lehmverkrustete Pfoten und acht

Mal trächtig im Haus, wie ein Nagetier, das ungestört wildert
In den Säcken mit Hühnerfutter. Wer es dann ist, gewiß, der

Spreizt sich, tapfer ausgezeichnet, wahrgenommen, aber nicht
Wirklich „verstanden", wie Wasser hell durchsichtig, aber zu

Fließend. So daß der Blickwinkel übermäßig weit, Taschen
Des Mantels nach außen gewendet in einem obszönen Akt.

11

Entire lexical fields beneath the tire tracks in the damp soil
Heard the track-vehicle convoys on bumpy roads

Hunches hiding in the reserves where expected, thus confirmed
Black fires smolder in the fog, tremors of the bumps in the road

Discharging ballast and the singed coat, time is protection
As with each furry animal, loam-caked paws and eight

Times pregnant in the house, like a rodent poaching undisturbed
In the sacks of chicken feed. Whoever it is then, certainly he

Is straddling, bravely distinguished, perceived but not
Truly "understood" like water clearly transparent but too

Fluid. So that the vantage point is excessively far
Coat pockets pulled inside out in an obscene act.

12

„Weiber und Kinder in die Sümpfe zu treiben
Hatte nicht den Erfolg, der wünschenswert gewesen

Denn die Sümpfe waren so tief nicht, daß
Ein Einsinken erfolgen konnte. Begaben sich

Ohne Widerstand zu den Exekutionsgräben
Faßten sich an den Händen, gingen gemeinsam

Zu den Rändern. Einige erkannten mich noch und
Riefen mir zu: Auf Wiedersehen, Herr Skubinn.

Gebe der Ordnung halber einen Durchschlag hinauf
Und kann nur hoffen, daß man uns ggf. unterstützt."

„Halte diesen Bericht als allenfallsiges Material
Für spätere Zeiten (Tarnungszwecke) recht gut."

12

"Driving females and children into the marshes
Did not succeed as would have been desirable

Because the marshes were not so deep that
Sinking in could occur. Proceeded without

Resistance to the execution trenches
Clasped each others' hands, went collectively

To the edges. Some still recognized me and
Called out to me: Good-bye, Mr. Skubinn.

Am sending a carbon copy ahead on account of the order
And can only hope that we have their support if needed."

"Deem this report quite good, at best material
For later times (purposes of camouflage)."

V

Kalkulation

Lawinenverschüttetensuchgerät

V

Calculation

Avalanche Rescue Device

1

Unmöglich, bei einem so dahinfegenden Wind
Die Nase zu erheben, Wimpern und Schnurrbart

Stalaktiten, das Innenohr schmerzzerrissen, Därme
Ein zuckendes Inferno. Schon lange sieht man Knie

Nicht mehr, versucht nicht an Zehen zu denken. Ohne
Telegraphenmasten, die eine vermutete Straße säumen

Wäre man verloren, aber auf welcher Seite der Pfosten
Die Piste – Nichtpiste ist Abhang. Was nicht sein darf

Lehrt nur der Sturz. Ernüchternd ist, wir sehen gar nichts
Keinen Gegner, keinen Vortrupp, wir sehen uns selbst

Undeutlich im Schneetreiben huschen und verwischen
Schließlich wie in einer Erdspalte eisigkalt versunken

Unser schweres Gerät

1

Impossible with such a sweeping wind
To lift your nose, eyelashes and mustache

Stalactites, the inner ear torn by pain, intestines
A twitching inferno. For a long time now the knees

Can't be seen, one tries not to think of the toes. With –
Out telegraph poles which line a presumed street

One would be lost, but on which side of the posts
The slope – non-slope is precipice. Only the fall teaches

What should not be. It gives us pause to see nothing at all
No enemy, no advance unit, we see ourselves

Faintly in the driving snow scurrying and blurry
Ultimately lost ice cold as though in a crevice

Our heavy gear

2

„Dieser Krieg widerspricht völlig dem Temperament der
Italiener, doch haben wir uns an Kot und Hinterlist gewöhnt

Wenn wir in der Ebene oder in offener Feldschlacht wären
Hätten wir die Österreicher längst mit Aplomb vertrieben

Auch unser Krieg ist hier, wie überall sonst, Stellungskrieg
Ein Kampf der gegenseitigen Abnützung, farbloser Krieg

Ein Kampf der Selbstverleugnung, Geduld und Zähigkeit
Flitter und der ganze Schmuck früherer Kriege vermißt

Sogar das Gewehr ist im Begriff, überflüssig zu werden.
Tagsüber ist man unter der Erde maulwurfartig vergraben

Nur bei Nacht etwas freier und unbekümmerter. Bomben
Und grelle Granaten suchen das Morgenlicht." Mussolini.

2

"This war completely contradicts the temperament of the
Italians, yet we have become accustomed to dung and deceit

If we were on the plain or in open battle, we would
Have long ago driven out the Austrians with aplomb

Our war is also here, like everywhere else, trench warfare
A struggle of mutual depreciation, colorless war

A struggle of self-denial, patience and tenacity
The spangle and ornament of earlier wars missed

Even the gun is about to become superfluous.
By day one is buried under the earth like a mole

Only at night somewhat freer and more lighthearted. Bombs
And glaring grenades seek the morning light." Mussolini.

3

Als wir in der Etappe waren, mit geöffneten Brusttüchern
Und sehr furchtsam auf unseren Rucksäcken saßen wie Leute

Die warteten, was mit ihnen geschehen soll am Ende der Welt
Das uns abgewandt war (von dem wir uns abgewandt früher)

Denn es gefiel nicht, wie weiter mit der Ausrüstung, fragten wir
Aber niemand antwortete und unter Kapuzen herumgeschleppt

Allerhand krauses Zeug, hirn- und sinnlos, Ballast abwerfen
Aktentaschen beim Angriff über den Kopf quer, man nahm uns

Die Hundemarken ab, die Leinen, wie Blechnäpfe schmeckten
Teller, *Thermoplast*, wo der Kopf stand, Verstand still nicht mehr

Verständiger Trost bis zum nächsten Mal. Stoffbeutel durchlöchert
Nie mehr würde brüderlich das Wort „brüderlich" geteilt werden.

3

When we were at the base with untied neckerchiefs
And sat very fearfully on our backpacks like people

Who waited for what would happen to them at the end of the world
Which had turned away from us (from which we once turned away)

For it was not pleasant, how to go on with the equipment, we asked
But no one answered and dragged around under hoods

All kinds of fuzzy stuff, brainless and senseless, discharging ballast
Briefcases covering our heads during the attack, they took off

Our dog tags, our leashes, plates tasted of tin bowls
Thermoplastic where the head was, mind no longer still

Sensible comfort until the next time. Cloth bag full of holes
Never again would the word "brotherly" be shared with brothers.

4

Nein, unsere Gegner lieben uns noch nicht, sie ertragen uns
Mit schlecht verhohlener Ergebung, stumme Feindseligkeit

Schnee füllt die Sandsäcke auf, versunkener Drahtverhau
Dahinter unförmig graue Bündel: die Toten vom anderen Tag

Warten nicht mehr, ob wir sie holen, ein Oberleutnant will
Daß wir es tun, was wir wollen, zählt nicht. Kein Darmkatarrh

Nicht die Fingerspitzen abfrieren, bevor aber ins Choleraspital
Dann doch lieber von einem 30.5 Projektil in tausend Fetzen

Sagte ich zu Robert, das Lager wie überzuckert von hellem Kalk
Schneeblätter Kleeblätter und eine todbleiche Nebelsonne, die

Auf Kristalle trommelt: gleißend, was für Menschen wir sind
Gähnen, teils aus Langweile und teils aus Hunger, das ist

Der Stellungskrieg

4

No, our enemies still don't love us, they tolerate us
With poorly concealed resignation, mute animosity

Snow fills up the sandbags, lost wire entanglements
Behind that, bulky gray bundles: the dead from the other day

No longer waiting for us to fetch them, a lieutenant wants us
To do it, what we want doesn't count. No intestinal catarrh

No freezing off the fingertips, but rather than to the cholera hospital
Then preferably into a thousand pieces by a 30.5 projectile

I said to Robert the camp was frosted over with bright lime
Snow leaves cloverleaves and a deathly pale foggy sun that

Drums on crystals: glistening, what kind of people we are
Yawning, partly out of boredom and partly out of hunger, that is

Trench warfare

5

Wenn wir ins Winterquartier ziehen, ein Zustand, den niemand wünscht
Und wenn wir im Winterquartier frieren wie Tiere, zum Kampf zu groß

Wenn wir das Winterquartier verkleinern (wie uns selbst), diese leidlich
Stumpfen Individuen, abhängig von Strohballen und Holz, Wärme, in die

Der Körper gewickelt wird hinter den Bildern, aber davon kein Wort
Wenn wir blaß, aber unerschüttert den Morgen loben und die Peiniger

Schweigen, wenn wir das Winterquartier quittieren im flirrenden Schnee
Und wir selbst hinter unseren gelassenen Brillen, fauchten wir, schlügen

Ein Kreuz, und wenn wir im Winterquartier Federn ließen, das ist der Fall
So oder so nicht: gibt genug Futter, Heubündel bereit, abends kommt eine

Mutter, legt Holz auf den Scheit. Wir zünden die Flamme, wir zünden und
Zündeln, alles im Nebel verfeuchtet das Holz und noch gar nichts bereit.

5

If we move into the winter quarters, a situation which no one wants
And if we freeze in the winter quarters like animals too big for battle

If we reduce the winter quarters (like ourselves), these tolerably
Dull individuals, dependent on bales of straw and wood, warmth into which

The body is wrapped behind the pictures, but not a word about that
If we praise the morning palely but unshaken and the tormentors

Are silent, if we abandon the winter quarters in the whirling snow
And we ourselves behind our serene spectacles, we would hiss, would cross

Ourselves, and if we left feathers in the winter quarters, that is the case
This way or not: there's enough fodder, bales of hay ready, in the evening

A mother comes, lays wood on the log. We light the flame, we light and
Ignite, everything in the fog dampens the wood and still nothing ready.

6

Die Stirn gebietet, sie gegen keine Mauer zu schlagen. Die Augen
Sprühn Funken im Körper, offene Geheimnisse, die niemand teilt

Nachrichtenlage (Heer) verworren und in den Höhlen vergraben
Vergeben wir uns nichts, vergraben zu einem stoischen Winterschlaf

Teilen sekundengenau Zeit steht still im Unterstand hinter Scharten
Gehen die Tiere unhungrig ihrem Pfleger nicht bis zum Hüftbeben

(Tigern sie?) geht das Trappeln der Hufe nicht auf die Nerven
Kotknödelchen und das Stirnbein fester als erwartet (Krater) nur

Haarriß: die Haut eine geduldige Hülle der üppigen Verzierungen
Des Hirns, wir denken uns Tierstille aus, die wir nicht fürchten

Marder und Stirnhöhlenbewohner, Hundegräber, Knochenleim=
Bottiche, Geheul, über dem windgepeitschte Fahnen knattern.

6

The brow demands not to be beaten against any wall. The eyes
Emit sparks in the body, open secrets which no one shares

Situation for (army) intelligence intricate and buried away in caves
We do not lose face, buried in for a stoic winter sleep

Sharing to the second, time stands still in the dugout behind loopholes
Do the animals come up to their keeper unhungry not until the hip shaking

(Do they prowl like tigers?) does the tramping of hooves not grate the nerves
Little dung dumplings and the frontal bone firmer than expected (crater) only

Hairline crack: the skin a patient shell of exuberant embellishments
Of the brain, we dream up animal stillness which we do not fear

Martens and frontal sinus occupants, dog graves, vessels with
Bone glue, howling above which windswept banners crackle.

7

Meldegänger, die sich ins Wetter hinauswagen, die Instrumente
Gehütet wie Schäfchen, rochen nach feuchter Wolle, auch Gras

Tiere, die den Pferch nicht ertrugen, drängten ins Freie, das so frei
Nicht lahm, geschoren und lammfromm. Witterung aufgenommen

Lachen und Heimleuchten wie blind stallwärts gewandt & sorgsam
Die Lämmerschwänze zittern gesehen, ja nur zittern gefürchtet

Als wäre Sehen Verstehen oder Verstehen ungesehen vor den Brillen
Die schattenlos sicher erblicken, was in eine ferne Gegenwart weist

Die dann vervielfacht ohne Mahnmal, Stelenfeld oder Feldstecher
Stachen in See in winzigen, nicht nennenswerten Booten, Westen

Luftgefüllt, das sind Möwen, auf Zufütterung wartend, Krumen, Nüsse
Mais. Oder: Was nicht eintraf, traf nicht. Flügelschlag. Schlag.

7

Harbingers who venture out into the storm, the instruments
Guarded like lambs, smelled of damp wool, also grass

Animals that couldn't bear the pen rushed into the open, so open
Not lame, shorn and lamblike. Scent of the prey picked up

Laughing and telling off blindly turned toward the stable & carefully
Lambs' tails seen trembling, indeed only afraid of trembling

As if seeing were understanding or understanding unseen before one's glasses
Which secretly behold that which can be seen in the distant present

Which then multiplies without memorial, stele field or field-glasses
Have set sail in tiny boats not worth mentioning, vests

Filled with air, those are seagulls waiting to be fed, crumbs, nuts
Corn. Or: What didn't arrive, missed. Flapping of wings. Flap.

8

Schematische Darstellung eines Schneebiwaks: 1 Schlafstelle
4 Kältegraben 2 Baustollen 5 Abstellfläche 3 Kochnische

Eingang im Windschatten, daß die verbrauchte Luft – 6 Kerze
Stroh oder ähnliches Material auf dem Boden, um keine Angst

Aufkommen zu lassen, aufgelassene Kochstelle: Erlaubnis der
Armee auch bei genügender Belüftung in einer geschützten Nische

Schnee blies in unsere Gesichter, wenn wir die kalte Hand hoben
War sie weiß. Biwaks auf der Schneedecke werden nur gebaut

Wenn die Schneedecke gering und Abdichtung nicht unmöglich
An der Decke eine Eisschicht, plane Luftlöcher an den Wänden

Kältegraben, Baustollen, Brandwache oder eine brennende Kerze
Prüft Kohlendioxydgehalt, allenfalls Alarm geschlagen wie zuletzt.

8

Schematic diagram of a snow bivouac: 1 sleeping compartment
4 cold trench 2 underground shelter 5 counter space 3 kitchenette

Entrance wind-protected for the stuffy air – 6 candle
Straw or similar material on the floor to allow no fear

To arise, cooking area left open: permission of the
Army also with sufficient ventilation in a secured niche

Snow blew in our faces, whenever we lifted the cold hand
It was white. Bivouacs are only built on the snow cover

Whenever the snow cover is slight and insulation possible
On the ceiling a layer of ice, air holes in the tent walls

Cold trench, underground shelter, fire watch or a burning candle
Tests carbon dioxide level, if necessary the alarm sounded like last time.

9

Zeitplane und Schneeblock allenfalls für zwei Mann, nicht zugeweht
Und darf kein anderes Isoliermaterial als unsere eigene Geschichte

Die schneeverweht und den Wärmeverlust schützend ausgleichen
Eine Kerze, solange sie brennt, enthält die Luft genügend Sauerstoff

Wenn aber – wie häufig geschehen – eine Verschlafenheit sowie
Blanke Trunkenheit, als hätte die Geschichte sich selbst belüftet

Nicht wirklich wahrscheinlich im Biwak bei heftiger Witterung
Wie deuten, daß unsere Gesichter verkniffen wirken mußten

Oder beleuchtet bläulichviolett, die Glieder gefühllos: hätten
Die Wärmeschichten anders den Biwak umhüllt, Brennstoff

Explosionsgefährlich ist nicht der einzelne Mensch gefährdeter
Entflammt flüssig über die eigene Gefährdungsfähigkeit hinaus.

9

Tarpaulin and snow block at most for two men, not blown shut
And no other insulating material than our own history, snowbound

May compensate protecting us from the loss of heat
A candle, as long as it burns, does the air contain sufficient oxygen

But if – as often occurs – drowsiness as well as
Sheer drunkenness, as if history had aired itself out

Not really probable in a bivouac in severe weather
How to interpret why our faces must have seemed wry

Or lit up bluish violet, the limbs without feeling: had
The layers of warmth enclosed the bivouac differently, fuel

Explosive isn't the individual human being more endangered
Will inflame fluidly in excess of his own capacity for endangerment.

10

Umsonst die Stimme gehoben mit Tremolo, umsonst das Zittern
Das Schlecken und Blecken, die ganze durchweichte Feuchtigkeit

Die Gabe des Überlebenden an den Toten, der sein Teil in Empfang
Nahm, als stände ihm etwas zu. Ehrfurcht gebietendes Schweigen?

Umsonst die Leitungen zerschnitten, auf Befehlsempfängern geritten
Gaskocher oder Kerzenstumpf, vereister Tod, der spurenlos kaltmacht

Umsonst dieses tropfende Glücksversprechen bis zum nächsten Mal
Und die Finger siegreich gespreizt, verwandelt, verschandelt der Bau

Vom letzten Jahr, in den Granaten schlugen. Perforierten die Wand
Ruinös gedacht bis zum Letzten, und was übrig, frißt kein Hund.

Angepeilt ist niemand, so tauchen wir unter die Zensur, tauchen
Und plustern uns auf: Schwäne sowie kriegswichtiges Federvieh.

10

In vain the voice lifted up with tremolo, in vain the trembling
The slurping and growling, the whole sodden dampness

The gift of the survivor to the dead man who received his part
As if he were entitled to something. Awe-inspiring silence?

In vain the lines were cut, ridden upon runners, gas cookers or
Candle stump, frosted death that bumps you off without a trace

In vain this dripping promise of happiness until the next time
And the fingers spread in victory, transmuted, the site mutilated

Last year when grenades fell. Perforated the wall
Destructively thought to the very end, and what's left no dog will eat.

No one was targeted, thus we plunge below the censor, plunge
And prance: swans as well as poultry of military importance.

11

Wenn dies ein Traum von Puschkin war: Mohrenkinder
Die sich mit Schneebällen bewerfen, bis Schnee sie bleicht

Wenn dies ein Traum: Brandwache, vielleicht Kältewache
An einem windgeschützten Ort Neuschnee gemessen mit

Einem Brettchen, was wir erlernten, war die Kälte des Herzens
Gleichgültig gegenüber den eigenen Zehen und fremden Körpern

Der Atem ist eine Maske, aufgesetzt und nie mehr ab, sonst
Wärmeverlust, schon eine einfache Wächte kann retten, was wir

Nicht kannten, war Unrettbarkeit, Luftlöcher in die Decke bohren
Darf nicht zugeweht werden, Tiefe des Schnees mit Sondierstangen

Gefühlt, Gaskocher, Notkocher der Armee sind erlaubt, Benzin nicht
Deshalb ein Kältegraben wie Windfang und Lichtschleuse zugleich

11

If this was a dream of Pushkin: Moorish children
Throwing snowballs at each other until snow bleaches them

If this a dream: fire watch, perhaps cold watch
At a wind-protected place fresh snow measured with

A slat, what we learned was the coldness of the heart
Indifferent toward one's own toes and foreign bodies

Breath is a mask, put on and never taken off, otherwise
Loss of heat, yet a simple snow drift can save, what we

Didn't know was irretrievable, drilling air holes in the ceiling
Not allowed to be blown shut, depth of the snow tested with probing poles

Gas cookers, army emergency cookers are permitted, not gasoline
Therefore a cold trench like porch and light security gate at the same time

12

Auf dem Saumpfad in blutigen Streifen war das gefrorene Hirn
Überrollt vom eisernen Reifen eines Wagens: erkennbare Spur

Eisbrocken, Schneeflocken, unaufhaltsame Historie der Kälte
Die begann, während die napoleonischen Truppen voraus und

Gingen auch frühere nach Osten uns voraus, geographisch weiter
Nicht korrigierbar: Nasenrot, Ohrenrot, Räusche der freien Luft

Kollabiert. Das Pferd, militärisch gesehen, ist der soldatischste Mensch
(Weiß es nur nicht, und soll es lebend im Tross nicht wissen) gestriegelt

Furcht versiegelt, weit über die Sümpfe hinaus ins zu Erobernde
Das dann in Etappen heruntergesiegt, hinterrücks vorwärtsverteidigt

Im Verfrorenen, dem keine Vorhut gewachsen, und der Finger am
Abzug eine kalte Wunde, ehe dann der Rückzug ungeplant beschämt

12

On the mule path in bloody stripes was the frozen brain
Rolled over by the iron tire of a carriage: recognizable track

Chunks of ice, snow flakes, incessant history of the cold
Which began while the Napoleonic troops advanced and

Also others advanced before us to the East, geographically further
Not correctable: nose redness, ear redness, frenzies in the open air

Collapsed. The horse, seen militarily, is the most soldierly human being
(Only doesn't know it and shouldn't know it living in the supply lines) curried

Fright sealed, far beyond the marshes out into the region to be conquered
Which then triumphed down in stages, defended forward from behind

In the deeply frozen land which no advance guard was up to, and the
       finger on the
Trigger a cold wound, rather than unplanned retreat in embarrassment

VI

Russische Obduktion

Pfützen

VI

Russian Autopsy

Puddles

1

Wenn ich nicht das Recht habe, den Tod zu wählen
Sagte sie, so habe ich immerhin das Recht, sagte sie auch

Ich habe das Recht, den Gegner zu wählen und den Ort
Und, sagte sie, ich habe das Recht, die Waffe zu wählen

Das sagte sie nicht, dachte es aber, je stärker der Gegner
Desto eher wirst du gebrochen. Es sei denn, du bist tot

Was auch keine Rolle spielt. Wenn du nicht tot bist, wähle
Aber nicht den Gegner, den Ort, die Waffe, wähle, was du nicht

Wissen kannst, sei nicht unschlüssig, zurückzutreten, als hättest du
Nicht gewählt, sie sprach wie eine betrunkene Russin, wässrige

Augen, alle Neigung und das Pathos gehörte den Schauspielerinnen
Aus Hollywood, nicht ihr, und wer nicht unter Vertrag stand, flog.

1

If I don't have the right to choose death
She said, I still have the right, she also said

I have the right to choose the enemy and the place
And, she said, I have the right to choose the weapon

That she didn't say, just thought it, the stronger the enemy
The sooner you are broken. Unless you are dead

Which also doesn't matter. If you aren't dead but don't
Choose the enemy, the place, the weapon, choose what you

Can't know, don't be irresolute about retreating as if you
Hadn't chosen, she spoke like a drunken Russian, watery

Eyes, all affection and pathos belonged to an actress in
Hollywood, not to her, and whoever wasn't under contract was fired.

2

Verträge sind nichtig, sind das Papier nicht wert, und abends
Genarrt von schwerfälligen Paragraphen, knallten die Absätze

Hüllen fielen, Körper in der Horizontalen, kreisende Becken
Nippel, Lichtreflexe, akuter Atemstillstand, leidlich reanimiert.

Was noch nicht tot war, inhalierte den Rauch und wußte
Was kam: nichts, das aber aus vollen Rohren, ein Waldbrand

War angeblasen, und keine Versicherung zahlte für Verlust, der
Vorgesehen, Sturm nahte, geschmacklos die Aussicht auf null

Ohne Nachsicht das Übereinanderfallen, das einen Namen hat
Wie Windhose, Wolkenzertrümmerung oder Äste bersten im Wald

Knirschend und gleichsam unüberhörbar. Scham, die entblößt
Furcht einflößt, schütter und bebend, klaffend unbelebt.

2

Contracts are void, aren't worth the paper, and in the evening
Mocked by cumbersome statutes, the high heels were clacking

Garments fell, bodies in the horizontal position, gyrating pelvises
Nipples, papillary light reflexes, acute apnea, tolerably reanimated.

What was not yet dead inhaled the smoke and knew
What was coming: nothing but with full strength, a forest

Was set ablaze, and no insurance paid for the loss which was
Foreseen, storm drew near, tasteless the prospect of naught

Mercilessly falling all over one another which has a name
Like whirlwind, cloud disintegration or branches cracking in the forest

Creaky and as it were unmistakable. Shame exposes
Fright infuses, thin and trembling, gaping inanimately.

3

Da, mit der Tasche aus Korbgeflecht war ich auf dem Markt
(Frag nicht, wie ich die Waffe beschaffte. Haltlose Geste.)

Und, sagte sie, ich habe Aprikosen gekauft, eine aufgeweichte
Tüte, aus der du essen kannst, iß, aber bedanke dich nicht.

Saft spritzt, das ist nur natürlich, wie Angst, die zu überwinden
Essen ist Verletzung, eine Blutung, pelzige, eingedellte Frucht

Da in der Tasche, aus der der Saft leckt – ich habe dir nur
Aprikosen gekauft, damit etwas geschieht, wenn du nicht ißt

Faulen die Früchte, und ißt du sie, dann ist das deine Gabe
Nicht deine Angst, im Ausguß meine Haare, seifenverklebt

Sagte sie, warum so streng, warum so fordernd, fragte er, warum
Deine Angst, probierte eine Frucht, und wohin mit dem Kern.

3

There with the handbag made of wicker I was at the market
(Don't ask how I got hold of the weapon. Unrestrained gesture.)

And, she said, I've bought apricots, a moist
Bag that you can eat from, eat but don't thank me.

Juice squirts, that's only natural, like fear to be overcome
Eating is injury, a hemorrhage, furry, bruised fruit

There in the bag the juice is leaking from – I only bought you
Apricots so that something would happen if you don't eat

If the fruits spoil and you eat them, then that is your gift
Not your fear, in the drain my hair, stuck together with soap

She said, why so harsh, why so demanding, he asked, why
Are you afraid, tried a piece of fruit, and where to put the pit.

4

Die Dummheit besteht darin, Schlußfolgerungen ziehen zu wollen
Schlußfolgerungen sind wie Wasserfälle, immer hinab hinab

Spritzend und sprühend, unsichtbar aufgespindelt Privatleben:
Vorläufig ja, aber umsonst. Die Frau, die an der Kasse eine Tüte

Packt, Schmuck im Nasenflügel, sonnengegerbte Brüste hart im Hemd
Das offensteht, damit man sie sieht, man sieht sie auch, wenn sie sich

Beugt in die Tüte, hart in der Hand, eine Stange Marlboro, ein Meßbecher
Nudeln, russischer Akzent, Nikotinzähne und weizenblond gefärbtes Haar

(Im Uralvorland gibt es ein Dorf, das Alpatovka heißt, zwei Greise
Mit zerschlissenen Wattejacken spielen hier noch die Moralapostel)

Ohne Besonderheit, so steht es im Paß, Touristenvisum für drei Monate
Dann nichts wie heim und wieder ohne Schlußfolgerungen zu ziehen.

4

Stupidity consists of wanting to draw conclusions
Conclusions are like waterfalls, always down, down

Squirting and spraying, invisibly forced private life:
Temporary, yes, but in vain. The woman at the counter who

Packs the bag, a nose ring, suntanned breasts firm in her shirt
Which is open so they can be seen, they can also be seen when she

Bends over the bag, firm in hand, a carton of Marlboros, a measuring cup of
Noodles, Russian accent, nicotine-stained teeth and wheat-blond dyed hair

(In the Ural foreland there is a village called Alpatovka, two old men
With tattered cotton jackets are still the upholders of virtue here)

With no distinguishing marks, as in the passport, tourist visa for three months
Then no place like home and again without drawing any conclusions.

5

Kleine Porzellanfiguren, die auf der Anrichte stehen, umfallen
Wenn einer schreit im Haus, es schreien viele, der Staatsanwalt

Bekommt für die Nacht ein Zimmer angewiesen, der Staatsanwalt
Spricht nicht, er ordnet Akten, das Zimmer karg. Mondweiße

Stableuchte, ein Ausguß mit einer Kalkkruste. Das war kein Verhör
Sondern Hinhören, Hinlangen: Aufpassen, schreien viele, das Haus

Ein Schwamm, bereit aufzunehmen, was noch aufzunehmen ist
Knarrende Treppe, das Geländer wacklig, ich dachte, sagte sie

Nicht an den Tod, eher an Leibesübungen in schwarzen Hosen
Und nackte Knie voller Schorf, der nicht mehr heilte und blieb.

In der Halle hatte man Blumengestecke und ein Kondolenzbuch
Aufgebahrt. Eine schüttere Kerze tropfte in ein besticktes Tuch.

5

Little porcelain figurines standing on the sideboard fall over
If anyone in the house screams, many are screaming, the district attorney

Receives a room allotted for the night, the district attorney
Does not speak, he is organizing files, the room sparse. Moon-white

Flashlight, a spout with lime crust. That was no interrogation but rather
Listening, reaching intently: paying attention, many are screaming, the house

A sponge, ready to absorb whatever is left to be absorbed
Creaking stairway, the banister wobbly, I didn't think, she said

About death, if anything about gymnastic exercises in black pants
And bare knees covered with scabs which no longer healed and remained.

In the hall flower arrangements and a book of condolence had been
Laid out. A thin candle was dripping onto an embroidered cloth.

6

Porzellanhunde, so hießen die Redefiguren, die ein Text lieferte
Beiläufig, wie Nippes, überflüssiges Zeug, hingestellt, damit

Die Zensur es kippte, über Bord warf, Scherben, Scherbengericht
Was die Zensur kippte, war nur ein Papiertiger, Porzellanhund

Genannt, höhnisch in Augenhöhe ordentlich hingestellt (Welpe?)
Damit ein anderer Satz (eine Figur) schattenhaft dunkel blieb

Auf unerfindliche Weise unentdeckt, schamvoll unverborgen
Da in der Tasche – ich habe dir Aprikosen gekauft, die faulen

Vor den sehenden Augen, alles wie Sitzen auf Friedhofsbänken
Kluft zwischen Wahrnehmung und Wissen verwischt, benutz

Den Verstand, sagen die Zensierten, aber nicht zu sehr, und sieh
Wie du die Angst überwindest, die Verletzung, die Blutung nicht.

6

Porcelain dogs, that's what the figures of speech were called in the text
Incidentally, like knickknacks, superfluous stuff, arranged in such a way that

The censor knocked them over, threw them overboard, shards, ostracism
What the censor knocked over was only a paper tiger, called

Porcelain dog, mockingly, neatly arranged at eye level (puppy?)
So that a different sentence (a figure) remained shadowy in the dark

Inexplicably undetected, unconcealed full of shame
There in the bag – I've bought you apricots, they will spoil

Before the visible eye, it is all like sitting on cemetery benches
Gap between perception and knowing eliminated, make use of

Your mind, those censored say, but not too much, and see
That you overcome your fear, the injury, not the hemorrhaging.

7

Alles war jetzt nichts, was war nicht, ein sowohl als auch nicht
War nicht gewählt, war nicht gequält, einmal vermählt worden

War ungeschützt verkehrt verliebt, geschnippelt und auf Anhieb
Verletzt (versetzt) und bodenlos gebettet auf sogenannte Stellen

Im hellen Licht des Tages eine Krimkatze in der Korbtasche
Geschmuggelt, das Fell elektrisch aufgeladen, der neunte Mai

Der Tag des Sieges rückte näher und wieder der Geruch nach
Hering und Arznei, Großvater polierte Orden und die Monde

Seiner Fingernägel, gut wäre, der Staat beerdigte ihn kostenlos
Mit einem Salut, er hatte nicht gewählt, also auch nichts falsch

Gemacht, Salut und frei von Sorgen bis zum Ural, die Uhr tickt
Bis morgen, eine Ansichtskarte mit einem Kreml, regenbogenbunt.

7

Everything was now nothing, what was not, an as-well-as-not
Was not selected, was not tormented, had once been wedded

Was unprotected inverted in love, snipped and straight away
Violated (dislocated) and abysmally bedded in so-called sites

In the bright light of day a Crimean cat smuggled in the wicker
Basket, its coat electrically charged, the ninth of May

The day of victory drew nearer and again the smell of
Herring and medicine, Grandfather polished medals and the moons

Of his fingernails, would be good if the state buried him for free
With a salute, he hadn't chosen, therefore also did nothing wrong

Salute and free of cares as far as the Urals, the clock is ticking till
Tomorrow, a picture postcard of the Kremlin, rainbow-colored.

8

Es ging nicht um die Sache, der Porzellanhund zerschmettert
Am Boden, der Großvater über die Scherben gebeugt, bewegt sich

Atmet, im Grunde geschieht sonst nichts bis zum Ural, alles mit
Einem gefrorenen Meer im Hintergrund sonst ohne Dekoration.

Wähle, was du nicht gewählt hättest, ohne wählen zu müssen
Eine junge, aber bereits übermäßig lebenserfahrene Frau

Dachte, sie läge auf dem Boden des Korbes, versifft zwischen
Fauligen Aprikosen, klopfte mit einem Dörrfisch ans Fenster

Niemand war da. (Im Ural gibt es ein Dorf, das Alpatovka heißt.)
Wirst es nie kennenlernen, sagt sie, wirbelnde Strudel und Flüsse

Hühner, eine staubige Hauptstraße, was auch keine Rolle spielt.
Wenn du nicht weggehst, wirst du gebrochen, anderswo auch.

8

It didn't involve this matter, the porcelain dog shattered
On the floor, the grandfather bent over the shards, is moving

Breathing, basically nothing else happens as far as the Urals, all with
A frozen sea in the background otherwise without ornamentation.

Choose what you would not have chosen without having to choose
A young woman, yet with an inordinate amount of life experience

Thought she would lie on the bottom of the basket, grimy between
Rotten apricots, would knock on the window with a dried fish

No one was there. (In the Urals there is a village called Alpatovka.)
You'll never go there, she says, to the swirling whirlpools and rivers

Chickens, a dusty main street which also doesn't matter.
If you do not go away, you will be broken, elsewhere as well.

9

Aprikosen gezuckert, die vernehmliche Stille der Nacht
Ausgeburt des Zwanges, Rückzug auf allen Ebenen

(Die unstatthaften eingeschlossen) wirst sie nie kennen
Lerne endlich kennen, sagte sie, mächtig aufgerichtet

Und dann wieder in Reih und Glied sich denkend
Bitte um Vergebung (schamvoll) und darauf einen Toast

All das kam von der gefrorenen Erde, dem beinharten
Denken um keinen Preis, nicht Luxus nicht Fülle wollen

Verzückung, sie hatte noch ein Kabel aufgerollt zu vergeben
(Schärfte das innere Ohr für die Stille, die später kommt)

Eine Steckdose war nicht vorhanden, Nacht, Luftschächte
Schiere Furcht auf den Leib gerückt, der dann blendend weiß.

9

Sweetened apricots, the audible silence of the night
Spawn of compulsion, retreat on all levels

(Those not allowed locked in) you'll never know them
Finally get acquainted, she said, powerfully upright

And then again in formation thinking to herself
Ask for forgiveness (full of shame) and then a toast

All that came from the frozen earth, the bone-hard
Thinking not for love nor money, wanting not luxury not plenty

Ecstasy, she had rolled up yet another cable to give away
(Sharpened the inner ear for the silence that comes later)

An electrical outlet was not available, night, air funnels
Sheer fright moved across the body, then dazzling white.

10

Vorbei. Heute braucht niemand die Schönheit zu begrüßen.
Vorbei auch die Zeit der Greise, die nie eine Ziege geklaut

Nie im Sumpf eingebrochen – der Staatsanwalt kann sich nicht
Beruhigen, der Abschnittsbevollmächtigte schweigt, Blick

Auf Kiefern. Keine Zeugen, keine Anklage, Akten vernichtet
Vorbei das Scherbenauflesen, Scherbengericht, alles verscherbelt

Das demütige Bücken, nicht mehr in Analogien gewatet
Wo einmal der Kopf gegen die Wand mit dem Porzellanhund

Zusammenstieß, wo Scherben nicht das winzigste Glück
Wo am Boden zerschmettert Gedächtnisstützen unterwegs

Flüchtige Schönheit wie wenig immer an alles grenzt –
(In zerschlissenen Wattejacken spielen Moralapostel Schach)

10

Over. Today no one needs to greet the beauty.
Over is also the time of old men who never stole a goat

Never broke into the swamp – the district attorney cannot
Calm down, the sector commissioner is silent, view

Of pine trees. No witnesses, no indictment, files destroyed
Over is picking up the pieces, ostracism, everything sold off

The humble stooping down, no longer wading in analogies
Where once the head collided with the porcelain dog

Against the wall, where shards not the tiniest bit of happiness
Where shattered on the floor memory aids on the way

Fleeting beauty like few things always borders on everything –
(In tattered cotton jackets the upholders of virtue play chess)

11

Narren, die den Verfall beklagen, deren Teil sie sind
Narren wie Geisterfahrer, abgewetzten Bremsbelägen gleich

Oder alle Aspirationen aufgegeben und gegen die Scheibe
Gehaucht, daß Eisblumen schmelzen nah vor der Stirn

Wo bin ich russisch, wo anders gestrickt, den Kopf voll
Von Gips und Knüllpapier, wo wenn nicht jetzt gebremst

Dem Verfall ergeben, ergeben auch das Dorf im Ural
Angespanntes Scharren der Schuhsohlen, Tee und Kuchen

Zu Ende gegessen, gekrümelt, wo bin ich wie russisch
Oder nicht am Ende zu Boden gestreckt, anders gestrickt

Die Schädel rasiert gleich allen Aspirationen hinlänglich
Und Birkenschößlinge, sturm- und niemals kniebedeckt.

11

Fools who bemoan the decay of that which they are part
Fools like head-on drivers, worn-away brake pads all the same

Or all aspirations given up and exhaled onto the wind –
Shield so that frost patterns melt close to the forehead

How am I Russian, of a different stripe, my head full
Of plaster and crumpled paper, how if not slowed down

Resigned to decay, also resigned the village in the Urals
Tense shuffling of shoe soles, tea and cake

Eaten up, crumbled, how am I like a Russian
Or in the end not knocked down, of a different stripe

The pates shaved all the same all aspirations sufficient
And birch saplings, storm- and never knee-covered.

12

Wir sind nicht hier, um zu entdecken, was nicht mehr
Zu entwirren, nur Verfall und Verwesung, *Prawda*-Papier

In der gegen Abend immer ruhiger atmenden Natur Pilze
Beeren und Benzinpfützen, Findlinge mit Nestflüchtern gepaart

Und verbeultem Geschirr. Fast hätte sie: Vollkommen! gesagt.
Sie hörte vom Wind das Rauschen, ich habe zu tun, ich warte

Vollkommen vergessen wie Brotkrumen, Hundekot, Bodennebel
Der Gegenwart, Dellen und Einbrüche, es ging um uns nicht

Ging, ging nicht, gesungen, war noch nicht losgegangen, ging nie
Vollkommen hinfällig die Knie, das schlecht gewaschene Gesicht

Mit den Händlern im Müll gewühlt, Pfandflaschen verscherbelt
Grausame Lieder. Wir hatten eine Aufgabe und erfüllten sie.

12

We are not here to discover what is no longer to be
Untangled, only decay and decomposition, Pravda-paper

In the ever-more-calmly breathing nature towards evening mushrooms
Berries and gasoline puddles, foundlings paired with precocial birds

And chipped dishes. She almost said: Perfect!
She heard the rustling of the wind, I am busy, I am waiting

Perfectly forgotten like bread crumbs, dog feces, ground fog
Of the present, dents and break-ins, it didn't concern us

Went, didn't go, sung, hadn't gone off yet, never went
Perfectly decrepit in the knees, the poorly washed face

Rummaged in the garbage with the dealers, refund bottles peddled
Dreadful songs. We had a mission and we accomplished it.

VII

Emotion

Rocksaumerhebung

VII

Emotion

Hiking up the Skirt

1

Nein, doch kein Schuldgefühl, Körpergewühl, Ekstase
Die sich schamhaft verbirgt im Nachhinein schutzsuchend

An Schamlippen gepreßt, über Hügel wandernd, mäandernd
Man muß die Füße in sicheren Schuhen energisch drehen

Gelenk, das knirscht, o du heilige Einfalt, Maronen geknackt
Im Herbst, nachdem das Fleisch sich vereinigt und auseinander

Wie Schuppen von den Augen fielen und erkannten sich selbst
Nackt und doch im Fell räudig, heiß gemacht – richtet sich

Nach dem Echo (Sensor), richtet den frostfreien Schlafplatz ein
Fledermaus, fliehendes Nachttier, seismographisch gut angepaßt

Aufgeschreckt, nein: keine Traurigkeit, eher ein Aufgebot
Von Energien, Schlieren, dies ist ja gewiß nur eine Äußerung

Wie: Wir doch nicht.

1

No, no guilty conscience, the tumult of bodies, ecstasy
That lies coyly hidden seeking shelter after the fact

Pressed on labia, wandering over hills, meandering
One must turn one's feet energetically in sturdy shoes

Joints that creak, oh blessed innocence, chestnuts cracked
Open in the fall, after the flesh has united and parted

Eyes were opened and revealed themselves to each other
Naked and yet mangy in the fur, made hot – conforming

To the echo (sensor), arranging the frost-free sleeping berth
Bat, fleeing nocturnal animal, seismographically well adapted

Alarmed, no: no sadness, rather a conscription
Of energies, streaks, this is surely just an expression

                    Like: Certainly not us.

2

„Ich merkte, wie mir die Hand locker wurde und ausrutschte
Wie mir der Verstand locker wurde, skrupelloses Denken

Das an Nichtdenken grenzte, milchige Grenzüberschreitung
Als ob" – doch die Lockerheit lockte nicht, was Einlochen

Gewesen wäre, war ein Auskochen und die lockere Hand
Stockte, zögerte, so war es nicht gemeint, alles, was nicht

Mein war, stand zur Verfügung. Hand, Fuß, Kopf, Bett=
Zipfel, wie dann der Rockbund locker saß zur Hüfte hin

Rutschte, darunter nackt, neu erfunden das Fleisch so weich
Knochenloses Denken, verdrehte Handgelenke, Seufzerglück

Das sich festbiß im bedenkenlosen Bindegewebe. Hand hob
Sich gegen wen, senkte sich. „Gedanklich stand ich im Freien."

2

"I noticed how my hand hung loose and slipped out
Like my mind hung loose, unscrupulous thinking

That bordered on non-thinking, milky frontier crossing
As if" – but the looseness was not alluring, what pocketing

Would have been was a concoction and the loose hand
Stopped, hesitated, it wasn't meant that way, everything that was

Not mine was available. Hand, foot, head, blanket flap,
Just as the skirt waistband then lay loosely at the hip

Slipped, naked underneath, newly discovered the flesh so soft
Boneless thinking, twisted wrists, sighs of happiness

That got bogged down in unhesitating connective tissue. Hand raised
Against whom, then lowered. "Intellectually I stood naked before God."

3

Wenn ich den Blick fest auf ein Ding richtete, Augenpaar, Besenstiel
Wäre ich sehr geehrt und überaus dankbar, eine Antwort zu erhalten

Stock, Rute oder Vogelscheuche, Leimrute, wenn der Blick nicht
Schweifte, locker ließe, Hindernisse suchte und Fahrkarten wie

Begrenzungen, Unüberwindliches, dann aber mit Schwung –
(Welches Ding dies sein könnte *passim*, war nicht ausgemacht)

Weichheit der Bewegungen verwischt und dann ins Gegenteil
Der Blick zu Boden, welche Kraftanstrengung wäre aufzubieten

Daß er bliebe in der Gegend der Geburt, nicht in der der Leisten
Und aus dem schräg gestellten Dachfenster fließt das Sehen

Haltlos in die Luft, ein Lachen, und eine Frau, ich, alles fängt
Erst an (ich widersage, sage), ginge durch das gewölbte Tor.

3

If I focused my gaze securely on one thing, pair of eyes, broom stick
I would be very honored and extremely grateful to receive an answer

Stick, rod or scarecrow, lime-twig, if the gaze did not
Waver, remained fixed, sought hindrances and tickets like

Limitations, the insurmountable, but then with zest –
(What thing this could be *passim* was not agreed upon)

Suppleness of movements blurred and then a complete switch
Gazing at the floor, what physical exertion could be mustered

For it to remain in the birth region, not in that of the groin
And from the slanting skylight window vision flows

Intangibly into the air, a laugh, and a woman, I, everything begins
Just now (I renounce, pronounce), would walk through the vaulted gate.

4

Und wärst du ein Kind gewesen, das ich geboren
Und wärst du ein Kind gewesen in meiner Obhut

Und hättest du Schutz gesucht (gefunden), der nicht
Geboten, aber verfügbar war seltsamerweise bei mir

Und du nähmst ihn in Beschlag und nistetest dich ein
Zaghaft in der schillernden Eihaut; Zellteilung, Zell=

Spaltung im ausgeforschten Organismus, dem nichts
Ferner liegt als. Herztöne und Blutströme, ein Pochen

Auf das Recht, geboren zu werden aus einer ungenannten
Frau und ein unverwandter Blick in die leisen Faltungen

Umhalsende Schnur, unanhaltbare Zeit, haltloses Wachsen
Das innehält, zurückgegeben zurückgegangen bist du.

4

And if you had been a child whom I bore
And if you had been a child in my custody

And if you had sought (found) protection which was not
Necessary but strangely enough was forthcoming from me

And you became engrossed in it and settled yourself in
Gingerly in the iridescent amnios; cell division, cell

Fission in the fully explored organism from which nothing
Is further than. Heart sounds and bloodstreams, a knocking

Upon the right to be born of a woman without
A name and an unrelated view of the gentle folds

Embracing cord, unstoppable time, unrestrained growth
That pauses, given back you have gone back.

5

Und wäre ich blitzlächelnd und stolz erweicht und zeigte
Dich und du kenntest nichts als meinen Arm (mein Herz)

Am Flaum zärtlich dich bergend, wärmend, die Stimme
Wie ein Tierlaut, schnurrend, gurgelnd und verhandelbar nie

Schneeflockenstimme, Heubündelstimme, Kufen, die ins Eis
Schneiden, jemand brach ein, aber nur bis zum Kniefälligen

Ich hätte dich wie einen klaren Gedanken ans Licht gebracht
Unter der schrundigen äußeren Rinde, die aufplatzte im Nu

Enten schnatterten und antworteten den Krähen nicht und wir
Auf der Brücke, so kreatürlich erschütterbar, doch auch frierend

Im Schnee, der schmilzt, und wir schmolzen, wärst du ein Kind
wärmte ich deine Hände, Füße, Ohren, aber. Das bist du nicht.

                                        Sagte sie.

5

And if I were beaming and proudly softened and showed
You and you knew nothing but my arm (my heart)

Tenderly hiding your peach fuzz, warming you, your voice
Like an animal sound, purring, gurgling and negotiable never

Snowflake voice, bale of hay voice, runners that cut into
The ice, someone broke in, but only as far as dropping to the knees

I would have brought you to the light of day like a clear thought
Under the crannied outer crust which burst open in a flash

Ducks were quacking and didn't answer the crows and we
On the bridge, such distressed creatures, but also freezing

In the snow that melts, and we melted, if you were a child
I would warm your hands, feet, ears, but. You are not.

                                        She said.

6

Wir sind nicht hier, um endlich etwas zu entdecken, sagte sie
Wir sind hier, um einen Eindruck zu bestätigen, der falsch ist.

Und wenn ich mich an meine Kindheit erinnere – Schweigen –
Dann eine übergroße Dunkelheit, verbeulte Platten, von denen

Gegessen wurde, alles auf den Tisch, was auf dem Tisch war
Wurde gegessen, Dunkelheit, Übelkeit (Trauer, sagte sie nicht).

Verdunklung war nicht das richtige Wort, keine Krähenschwärme
Verdunklung setzte den Sinn für Helligkeit voraus, Scheinheiligkeit

Den sie nicht kannte. Wörter waren Wärter, auch Hellhörigkeit war
Ein Gewinn wie Wintergewitter, Blitze und Ameisen im Bad, sagte sie

Oder Nager, Säuger, alle Tiere, die ich nicht kennenlernen durfte
Sagte sie, oder nur in steil selbsterschaffenen Momenten, wie eben.

6

We are not here to finally discover anything, she said
We are here to confirm an impression that is false.

And when I recall my childhood – silence –
Then oversized darkness, chipped plates that

We ate from, everything on the table, whatever was on the table
Was eaten, darkness, nausea (she didn't say mourning).

Darkening was not the right word, no swarms of crows
Darkening presumed a sense of lightness, hypocrisy

That she did not know. Words were guards, clairaudience was also
A benefit like winter storms, lightning and ants in the bath, she said

Or rodents, mammals, all animals that I wasn't allowed to get to know
She said, or only in abruptly self-created moments like right now.

7

Durch alle Turbane und Hinhaltungen hindurch, gegürtet mit
Richtlinien und verbürgten Gewißheiten bis zum letzten Loch

In undenklicher Rückenlage nimmt sie in Empfang, was ihr
Zusteht, den Samen Amen, den leichten Druck der Schenkel

Geschaukelt im Geist des Schweißes, Spermas mit Worten
Geblasen im Sandsturm der Wüste, im Mund aufgefangen

Den Atem, den Schweiß, den Samen noch einmal, wie
Fernrohre sich auf einen Kometen richten, und der Komet

Ist nie Fleisch geworden vom eigenen Bein abgesegnet
Sei unser Denken und Schenken, die prallen Ergüsse naß

Verwischt ins Haar. Ob es sich um neuen Besitz handele
Fragte sie. Oder eine verpflichtende Schenkung zeugt aus ihr.

7

Throughout all the turbans and holdouts, girded with
Directives und guaranteed certainties up to the last hole

In immemorial supine position she takes what she is
Entitled to, the semen amen, the light pressing of the thighs

Swayed in the spirit of sweat, of sperm with words
Blown in the sandstorm of the desert, caught in the mouth

The breath, the sweat, the semen once again, like
Telescopes aimed at a comet, and the comet

Is never made flesh by one's own leg blessed
Be our thinking and giving, the tense discharges wet

Smeared in the hair. Whether it involves a new possession
She asked. Or a compulsory donation stems from her.

8

Die Körper haben sich in die Leiber zurückgezogen
Bebende Tiere sind sie ohne Fell und Pfotenabdruck

Ahnen, daß nicht alles Körper, was fingernagelklein
Taubeneigroß unter der Membran pochend hervortritt

Glitzernd und schillernd zur Brunftzeit gerüstet, Atem
Der stocken macht, Flimmerhärchen, Taubnesselturteln

Hand arbeitete, stimulierte Muskeln, hob sich gegen wen
Zottig zerzaust das Schamhaar eine Mähne, Ringfinger

Erigiert, saßen zu zweit in der Aufnahmekanzlei, zitternd
Und flehend. „Warum fehlt Ihr Krankenkassenchip, bitte?"

Wasserzeichen nicht wahr, wie dann im Fruchtwasser
Paddelnd schniefend durch Hecken und kleine Dickichte.

8

The bodies have withdrawn into their physical shells
They are trembling animals without fur or paw prints

To sense that not all bodies are small as a fingernail
Large as a dove's egg emerge throbbing under the membrane

Glistening and iridescent primed for the rutting season, breath
That makes you stumble, cilia, turtle-doving sweet dead nettles

Hand was working, stimulating muscles, raised up against whom
Raggedly unkempt the pubic hair a mane, ring finger

Erected, sat as a pair in the admission office, trembling
And beseeching. "Why is your health insurance card missing?"

Watermark isn't it, like in amniotic fluid then
Paddling sniffing through hedges and small thickets.

9

Er wollte nun schon fast nichts mehr sagen (saugen) wollte
Sich retten, gerettet werden, ein klammer Klinikinsasse

Dem eine Schwester eine sanfte Hand auflegt, die kühlt
Einschreibung in das Gedächtnis des Körpers wie starke

Medikamentierung, richtete sich ein im Wortfeld „Lust"
(Läufig? Beweglich?) eher als Urlaut mißverstanden

In Löffelform gegossen und nicht aufgerichtet, Muskel=
Verkürzung, was Lärm macht, macht Lust, macht der Mai

Muß reich an Bäumen sein, eine geschützte Baumgruppe
Regelmäßig beschnitten, so daß die Krone fächerförmig

Aus der ein Lockruf zu seiner eigenen Unterhaltung
Im Wald (klingt vielmehr rauh und etwas gellend im Ohr)

Brutvogel: der weißbestrumpfte Fuß

9

He didn't have anything more to say (suck) wanted
To save himself, to be saved, a clammy clinic patient

Upon whom the nurse lays a gentle, cooling hand
Inscription in the memory of the body like strong

Medication, settled himself into the lexical field of "desire"
(In heat? Flexible?) more likely misunderstood as a primal sound

Poured out into a spoon and not raised up, muscle
Contraction, whatever makes noise, makes desire, is made by May

Must be rich in trees, a protected grove of trees
Regularly pruned so that the crest is fan-shaped

From which a birdcall for his own entertainment
In the forest (sounds rather hoarse and shrill to the ear)

        Brooding bird: the white-stockinged foot

10

Zahnersatz Angstbesatz „nimm doch die Hände vom Mund"
(Der ein Schlund war, aber nicht verschlang) als ich es sicher

Sagen konnte, der Kopf so hängerisch wie Efeuranken wie
Gebären und Gebärde: naturwüchsiger Zusammenhalt

Abschilferung, die kein Einnisten erlaubt, aber erhofft
Wissensstand und schwankendes Rohr im Wind, so

Trügerisch kein vergleichendes Wie! Jedes Wort hat Luft=
Wurzeln, und wo bin ich, die ich hier kopflos steh, wo

Sind die Füße, wie angelt der Arm nach dem Ast, und wo
Sind die kräftigen Ranken des Efeus, wenn die Mauer

In deren Ritzen er wurzelt, fällt. Haltlosigkeit, auch Gärtner=
Stolz ist ein Wort, zu Kreuze kriechen, klingt wie Standpauke.

10

Denture edge of fear "take your hands from your mouth"
(Which was a gullet but did not guzzle) when I could say it

With certainty, my head hanging like ivy tendrils like
Birthing and gesturing: naturally formed coherence

De-reeding that allows for no nesting yet desires it
State of knowledge and swaying pipe in the wind, so

Deceptive no comparative Like! Every word has aerial
Roots, and where am I that I stand here headless, where

Are my feet, how does my arm fish for the branch, and where
Are the sturdy tendrils of ivy, if ever the wall will fall

In whose cracks it is rooted. Instability, also gardener's
Pride is a word, eating crow, sounds like a rebuke.

11

Alle Seglerarten haben wenig Feinde, Zwergsegler
Die ihre Beute verdaut oder bis zur Unkenntlichkeit

Zerdrückt vertilgt, schnelles Schnabelgeschnatter und
Flugträume von Invasoren, die aus der Luft stechend

Fallen und zerschellen, so daß die Eierschalen wie im
Mörser zerdrückt, entrückt, doch mit Folie überzogen

Schwankend und flatternd auf dem Boden so unsicher
Wirken orientierungslos, kläglich die Luft entbehrend

Demjenigen, der gewohnt, auf die Stimmen von Vögeln
Zu achten, fällt diese wohlklingende Lockstimme auf

„Güb ga güb güb ga güb", die beiden Geschlechtern
Zu eigen, Singsang und Einklang, sehnsüchtige Litanei.

11

All species of swallows have few foes, dwarf swallows
Which digest their prey or devour them, crushed

Beyond recognition, quick chattering of beaks and
Dreams of flying from invaders coming from the air

Fall and crash so that, like in a mortar, the eggshells
Are crushed, carried away, yet covered with foil

Swaying and fluttering on the ground so uncertain
Appear disoriented, miserably doing without air

To one who is accustomed to paying attention
To the birds' voices, this melodic mating call is striking

"Coo ca coo coo ca coo," which is typical of
Both sexes, singsong and unison, yearning litany.

12

Ich bin die Stimme nicht, die spricht, wer spricht
Ein Laubbaum läßt die Blätter fallen, wer spricht

Ich bin gebrochen, bin gekrochen, ich brach selbst
Und sprach: die Vögel sind zu schwer zum Fliegen

Wir fliegen nicht, wir üben und darüber fallen wir
Wir krauchen, aber wissen nicht, was aufrecht war

Es gibt so viele Meteore, die dann verglühn. Ich bin
Wie Steine, die man nicht aufliest in den Straßengräben

Grußformelleicht bin ich es nicht, die augenblicklich spricht
Ich höre Blätterstürmen, Wind, hole Gesprochenes wieder

Wiederhole Unausgesprochenes und wird mein Rocksaum
Herabgelassen im Frühjahr und fällt noch einmal Schnee.

12

I am not the voice that speaks, who is speaking
A shade tree lets its leaves fall, who is speaking

I am broken, have crept, I've broken myself
And spoken: the birds are too heavy to fly

We do not fly, we practice and we trip over that
We creep but do not know what was upright

There are so many meteors that then fade away. I am
Like stones that one doesn't pick up in roadside ditches

Lighthearted as a greeting it is not me momentarily speaking
I hear storms of leaves, wind, retrieve what was spoken

Repeat the unspoken and will the hem of my skirt
Be let down in the spring and will snow fall once again.

VIII

Okkupation

Rauschkonkurrenz

Und schaut die geäderten Lider von Toten an („Es ist nur Rauch
Der aus uns rinnt.") Punkt. Raum. Rauhreif. Feld. Wegwarte. Ort.

VIII

Occupation

Competing interference

And just look at the veined lids of the dead ("It is only smoke that
Pours out of us.") Period. Space. Hoar-frost. Field. Chicory. Place.

1

Ein wild zu allem entschlossener Weltbesttorhüter
Steigt die Stufen der Freitreppe empor, strahlend

Steht er an der Balustrade mit der Trophäe in der Hand
Belagerungszustand oder Infiltration, das Gedächtnis

Eine Rumpelkammer mit zu entsorgenden Despoten
Unsicher im Schritt hineingeschleudert, aber breitbeinig

Geballter Einsatz hebt ihn hoch ins Blitzlichtgewitter
Belagerungszustand folgt der Invasion, gedachte Siege

Reichen ins Aus. Landesfarben glühn über zwei Männern
Die einen dritten mit sich schleifen, der tot ist noch nicht

Nicht einmal nackt: „Der ist es, der oder keiner." Den
Straft niemand Lügen nicht mehr keine Fahne halbmast.

1

The world's best goalie wildly determined to do anything
Climbs up the steps of the front stairway, beaming

He stands at the balustrade with the trophy in his hands
State of siege or infiltration, his memory

A junk room with despots to be disposed of
Pitching in, unsteady in stride but straddling

Concentrated activity lifts him high into the storm of flashbulbs
State of siege follows the invasion, imaginary victories

Go out of bounds. National colors glow above two men
Who are dragging a third one along who is not quite dead

Not even naked: "That's him, him or it's nobody." Him
No one punishes for lying any more no flag half-mast.

2

Die wir zu unseren Feinden gemacht hatten leichtfertig
Erbaten sich Waffenruhe und Schonung, wir gewährten sie

Das war in den Augen der Weltöffentlichkeit eine gute Sache
Die Zivilbevölkerung blieb in Löchern, getrockneter Schlamm

Und zerbeulte Bratpfannen, hart zusammengebackener Unrat
Zwischen Einschußlöchern und Moniereisen, so mußte man

Ihre Behausungen nennen, wir lümmelten neben den Panzern, die
Tieren gleich über unsere knatternd beflaggten Zeltstädte wachten

Während Hühner golkernd und torkelnd Kotflügel erklommen
Statisten, mit Milben übersät, wir hätten ihnen den Hals um –

Kleinkinder hoben den schlaffen Blick, nickten ein, wimmernd
Das Fieber hatte ihre Lippen gedörrt, der Geruch von Unschuld

Wich.

2

Those whom we had frivolously made into our foes
Requested a ceasefire and clemency, we granted it

In the eyes of the world public that was a good thing
The civilian population remained in holes, dried mud

And battered frying pans, hard caked-on rubbish
Between bullet holes and reinforcing bars one had to

Name their dwellings, we lolled next to the tanks which
Watched over our fluttering flagged tent camps like animals

While chickens clucked and careened climbing up fenders
Passersby, blotched with mites, we should have wrung their –

Small children raised their droopy gazes, dozed off, whimpering
The fever had parched their lips, the smell of innocence

Gave way.

3

Was wir aus der Waffenruhe herausschlugen, hatte einen
Namen: bedingungslose Kapitulation. Feuerwerke krachten

Uns um die Ohren, wir brachten Wasser in Plastikkanistern
Flickten zerborstene Leitungen, verteilten Fruchtdrops an alle

Decken und Impfserum, Gleichzeitigkeit von Verderben und
Glücklicher Fügung, aus unsren schnürgesenkelten Stiefeln triefte

Kalter Schweiß, wir wollten den Angstgeruch vergessen, egal
Wer ihn ausströmte, Rauschkonkurrenz und gegrillte Leitungen

Vergaßen uns selbst als Befehlsempfänger, wuchsen über uns
Hinaus, als wären wir andere bei der Invasion gewesen als jetzt

Waren wir Lagerfeuerleute, angefacht, fauchten wir zurück
Erkannten unsere Stimmen ähnlich blechernen Trompeten

3

That which we had gained in the ceasefire had a
Name: unconditional surrender. Fireworks crashed

All around us, we brought water in plastic canisters
Fixed burst water lines, handed out fruit drops to everyone

Blankets and vaccine serum, synchronicity of decay and
Stroke of luck, from our string-laced boots oozed

Cold sweat, we wanted to forget the smell of fear, regardless
Of whence it came, competing interference and grilled wires

Forgot ourselves as order-takers, exceeded our expectations
As if we had been different during the invasion than now

Were we campfire people, stoked, we hissed back
Realized our voices were akin to tinny trumpets

4

Es ist besser, etwas zu tun und zu sterben, sagten die Besiegten
Die Besetzte waren, und wir saßen auf ihren Plätzen, Mädchen

Großäugig und biegsam (sie schickten die schönsten) brachten
Gläser mit Tee, unser Trinken war diplomatisch, wir nippten nur

Es ist besser, nichts zu tun und das Sterben abzuwarten, sagten sie
Auch. Seuchen kamen und gingen nicht mehr, wir mit Mundschutz

Schwiegen. Fieber wütete. Wir sahen die Mädchen, wir faßten sie an
Wir faßten Mut, daß die lebendigen Körper gegen tote aufzurechnen

Wir waren Teil einer Geschichte, die oben und unten nicht kannte
Kannten die Mädchen mit Namen, und sie kannten uns bald inwendig

Und auswendig, warfen sich uns brünstig an den nackten Hals
Körper an Körper in einem arbeitsamen Takt und waren erledigt

Danach.

4

It is better to do something and to die, said the conquered
Who were the occupied, and we sat at their places, girls

Large-eyed and supple (they sent the most beautiful) brought
Glasses with tea, our drinking was diplomatic, we only sipped

It is better to do nothing and to wait for dying, they also
Said. Epidemics came and no longer went, we with masks

Were silent. Fever raged. We saw the girls, we took hold of them
We took courage that the living bodies could offset the dead ones

We were part of a story which knew no beginning or end
Knew the girls by name, and they soon knew us inwardly

And outwardly, threw themselves passionately at us
Body to body at a painstaking rhythm and were worn out

Afterwards.

5

Nicht bei seinen Handlungen, sondern schon bei künftigen Plänen
Dem Feind rigide entgegentreten, sich in ihn versenken, als wäre

Man selbst der unsichtbare Feind oder sein sichtbarer Stellvertreter
An den Börsen der Welt jubelten Wasserträger und Waffenlieferanten

Wurden wir außerbörslich gehandelt nach einer Logik des Fertigen
Die verheißungsvoll vibrierte oder war Handeln längst umgekippt

Die Spekulanten, die Zuträger waren auf unserer Seite wie besoffen
Von uns eingenommen waren wir selbst, bekränzt und beschämt

Durchbohrung, Enteignung des Körpers, Zeitalter der Nachfahren
Und Erben, heldisch gebrauchter Waffen oder wie Aischylos dichtete:

„So sprach der Adler, als er an dem Pfeile, der ihn durchbohrte
Das Gefieder sah: So sind wir keinem anderen erlegen als unserer

Eigenen Schwinge . . .“

5

Not in his actions, but already in his future plans
Stiffly facing the foe, becoming absorbed in him, as if

Oneself were the invisible foe or his visible representative
Water-carriers and arms dealers cheered the world's stock markets

Were we treated over the counter according to the finisher's logic
Which vibrated with promise or had trade been overturned long ago

The carpetbaggers, the informers were on our side like drunks
We were absorbed in ourselves, wreathed and ashamed

Penetration, dispossession of the body, the age of descendants
And heirs, heroically used weapons or as Aeschylus wrote:

"Thus spoke the eagle when he saw the feathers on the arrow
That pierced him: Thus we succumb to no one other than our

                              Own pinion..."

6

Reicht man den Besiegten die Hand, leidet sie Schaden dabei
Oder ist die Hand bedenkenlos siegreich gereicht ein Zeichen

Daß dies nur ein Anfang sei von was, daß die gereichte Hand
Die ergriffene umfaßt, daß ausreichende Maßnahmen und Gaben

Nicht genügen, aber was folgt daraus, andere drehen sich um
Auf dem Absatz, Abbruch der nicht angefangenen Beziehung

Ist die gereichte Hand nur Anfang einer zukünftigen Umarmung
Die im Keim erstickt die gereichte Hand wie verrückt drückt

Daß morgen und vorgestern Trümmer und Trümmerbrüche
Und die Schrapnellwunden auf Hauswänden und der Gestank

Aus den Kellern, die Hände infiziert, auch die Verweigerung
Des Händedrucks, vielfach praktiziert, entehrt den Verweigerer.

6

If one shakes hands with the conquered, do those hands suffer damage
Or is the hand extended in victory without hesitation a sign

That this is only the beginning of something, that the extended hand
Envelopes the clasped one, that adequate measures and gestures

Do not suffice, but what comes of that, others turn their backs
On their heels, abandonment of the relationship not begun

Is the extended hand only the beginning of a future embrace
Nipped in the bud the extended hand presses like crazy

That tomorrow and the day before yesterday rubble and fractures
And the shrapnel holes in house walls and the stench

From the cellars, hands infected, also the refusal of the
Handshake, practiced many times, dishonors the objector.

7

Hat man die Hand gereicht als Komplize des Untergangs
Der Besiegten oder als Unterpfand einer zukünftigen Welt

Nachdem wir handgreiflich Krieg geführt hatten, Angst
Hatten wir jetzt, daß unser Sieg unter den Händen zerstob

Die fremden Toten setzten sich in unserem Gemüt fest
Fraßen an unserer Lebendigkeit, drückten nieder, waren

Wir Einzelne, atomisiert nach dem Sieg, heimwehkrank
Und der Rausch war vorbei, die Angst war bombenfest

Grundlos war sie nicht, wo wir patrouillierten, gähnten
Krater, Straßensperren an jedem Stadttor, in einem Karren

Verborgen könnte eine Waffe sein aus unserem Bestand
Drehten Melonen einzeln um, lachhaft, getötet zu werden

                                        Gerade jetzt

7

Did one shake hands as an accomplice to the downfall
Of the conquered or as a pledge to a future world

After we had violently waged war, we were
Fearful now that our victory had dispersed

The unknown dead became firmly entrenched in our minds
Devouring our vitality, weighing us down, were we

Individuals, atomized after the victory, homesick
And the interference was past, fear was dead certain

It wasn't unfounded, wherever we patrolled craters
Gaped, roadblocks at every city gate, in a cart

A weapon could be concealed from our supplies
Turned melons over one by one, laughable to be killed

Just now

8

„Die Soldaten kommen & beraten, was mit mir zu tun sei.
(Alle bezeugten Vorgänge sind protokollarisch bestätigt.)

Die Soldaten würfeln, räsonieren, ob ich vor ihnen hinkrache
Einer schlägt vor: Man tritt ihm beim Hofspaziergang

Drastisch auf den Fuß, bis der Gefangene aufspringt auf=
Schreit. Das wäre ein Fluchtversuch. Die anderen stimmen zu.

Als ich das Zimmer verlasse, in meine Zelle zurückgeführt
Folgen mir die Soldaten mit demütigenden Schmähungen.

Du Schuft. Du Lump. Die Kugel ist schon für dich gemacht.
Nur der Aufseher verhindert das Eindringen der Soldaten

In den Zellengang, den ein schweres Eisengitter abschließt, ja
Nur das energische Eingreifen des Aufsehers verhindert –"

8

"The soldiers come & discuss what should be done with me.
(All attested procedures are documented for the record.)

The soldiers roll the dice, argue if I will crack in front of them
One suggests: one of us should stomp on the prisoner's foot so hard

When he walks through the courtyard that he jumps up cries out.
That would be considered an attempt to flee. The others agree.

As I leave the room, led back to my cell
The soldiers follow me with humiliating taunts.

You scoundrel. You rascal. A bullet has your name on it.
Only the head guard prevents the intrusion of the soldiers

Into the prison hallway, closed off by heavy iron grating, yes
Only the active intervention of the head guard prevents –"

9

„Ich sah nur das Rechteck aus Maschendraht, dahinter
Wie ein aufgespießter Schmetterling, den Mann festgehakt

An der Schlinge des Zauns. Als er mich sah, Allmächtiger
Ein aufgerissenes Gesicht, Hände über den Kopf erhoben

Augenbraue mit Blut verkrustet und die Lippe gespalten
Aber vor dem Heben müssen die Hände klammheimlich

Die Waffe gespannt haben, eine Waffe, die ich nicht sah
(Aber zu spüren glaubte). Stop, rief ich, stehenbleiben

Die Hände sanken, fuchtelten, nestelten, ehe ich merkte
Was ich nicht glauben konnte, schoß ich so daß es spritzte

Aus dem Kopf unerwartet, zog mich zurück zur Meldung.
Dies ist mein geschönter Bericht, so wahr mir Gott helfe."

9

"I saw only the rectangle made of wire netting, behind that
Like a transfixed butterfly, the man hooked up on the mesh

Of the fence. When he saw me, almighty God
A gaping face, hands raised above his head

Eyebrow encrusted with blood and the lip split
But before being raised the hands clandestinely

Must have cocked the weapon that I didn't see
(But thought I sensed). Stop, I yelled, don't move

The hands fell, waving about wildly, fumbling, before I noticed
What I couldn't believe, I shot in a way that made his head

Spatter unexpectedly, withdrew to report it.
This is my sugarcoated report, so help me God."

10

Viele Piloten werden sehr empfindlich, sie gehören nicht zu uns
Binden sich niemals an den Ort, an dem man sie stationiert

Die Royal Air Force lebt in den riesigen Hangars der Luftwaffe
Igelt sich mit ihren Maschinen ein, sie haben von Deutschland

Geträumt wie von einer blutgedüngten Wüste, kein Dom mehr
Keine Bahnhöfe, keine Runen, sie sprechen ihren eigenen Slang

Fühlen sich erhaben über alle, Bodentruppen und Nachschub:
Flieger sind sie und bleiben's, unsere notdürftige Verwaltung

Ist ihnen ein Dorn, auf kratzigen Tonträgern hören sie Musik:
„Erst machen wir uns die Mühe, zerstören deutsche Städte

Dann kommt ihr mit eurer Militärregierung, allen Schikanen
Pflastert und päppelt die Deutschen wieder auf." Kopfschütteln.

10

Many pilots become very sensitive, they are not our kind
Never become attached to the place where they're stationed

The Royal Air Force is housed in the gigantic Luftwaffe hangars
Burrows in with machines, they have dreamed of Germany

As a desert fertilized with blood, no longer any cathedrals
No train stations, no runes, they speak their own slang

Feel superior to everyone, ground troops and reinforcements:
They are airmen and always will be, our makeshift administration

Is a thorn in their sides, on scratchy albums they listen to music:
"First we make every effort to destroy German cities

Then you come along with your military government, all the trimmings
Pave the roads and build up the Germans again." Heads shaking.

11

Alles war schwerer in der besetzten Stadt, als wir erwarteten
Wir sahen zurück, sahen uns im düsteren Licht, trinken half

Nicht wirklich. Auch die Hände waren bleischwer geworden
Hände in den Schoß, die Besiegten ließen uns machen, zeigten

Daß sie uns übersahen in der veruntreuten Nacht Ausgangssperre
Wasserleitungen rauschten, Karren brachten Früchte und Munition

Die wir konfiszierten. Nahmen uns, was uns gefiel, so wurden wir
Wählerisch. Regnete es, rochen wir den Brandgeruch des Holzes

Besser: es regnete auf Steine als auf einen geschwärzten Dachstuhl
Wir waren die Ordnung der Steine, durchstreiften die Stadtviertel

Waren der Ordnung überdrüssig, der wir beidhändig unterworfen
Fühlten uns von uns selbst kontrolliert vorläufig und zukünftig

11

Everything was more difficult than we expected in the occupied city
We looked back, saw ourselves in the gloomy light, drinking didn't

Really help. Our hands too had become heavy as lead
Hands in our laps, the conquered had us do things, showed

How they ignored us in the embezzled night curfew
Water pipes roared, carts brought fruit and munitions

That we confiscated. Took what we wanted, so we became
Choosy. When it rained, we smelled the burning wood

Better: it rained on stones as on a blackened roof-truss
We were the regime of stones, roved through the districts

Were weary of the regime which we were subject to with both hands
Felt we were controlled by ourselves for the present and in the future

12

Sicher waren wir nicht, wir vermuteten eine Plünderin oder
Etwas fiel ab: das Zeichen der Namenlosigkeit, Nachtsichtgeräte

Wir sahen jede Bewegung beleuchtet und waren im Dunkeln
Etwas fiel ab: die Scham, nicht getötet worden zu sein oder –

War es eine Schwangere, die, als hätte sie ihn gerade gestohlen
Einen Topf versteckte an ihrem Leib. Als wir sie festnahmen

Schrie sie, schrie sie so laut, Saures quoll aus dem Blechtopf
Auf den Stein, uns ekelte, das Gefühl für Ekel war nicht betäubt –

Vor dem Flüssigen, wie Blut schleimig oder geronnene Suppe, wir
Nahmen nicht einmal den Topf, nahmen sie nicht in Gewahrsam

Nahmen uns selbst nicht wahr als Hüter einer zukünftigen Ordnung
Was nicht abfiel: Sichelmond und eine bleiche Milchstraße darüber.

12

We were not safe, we suspected a female looter or
Something fell: the sign of namelessness, night vision equipment

We saw every movement lit up and were in the dark
Something fell: the shame of not having been killed or –

Was it a pregnant woman, who, as if she had just stolen it
Concealed a pot under her dress. When we arrested her

She screamed, screamed so loud, gunk gushed out of the steel pot
Onto the stone floor, we were disgusted, our disgust wasn't numbed –

Faced with the liquid, slimy like blood or curdled soup, we
Didn't even take the pot, didn't take her into custody

Didn't perceive ourselves as protectors of a future regime
What didn't fall: crescent moon and a pale galaxy above it.

IX

Wilde Spekulation

die andere Seite

IX

Wild Speculation

the other side

1

Niedere, wie verkabelte Mauern, angeknabbertes Grün
Lange, nichtssagende Gebäude, könnten Kasernen sein

Oder eine Hundezucht im großen Stil, wir wiederum
Meinten, Tiere vermehrten sich von selbst, brauchten

Weder Hundezüchter noch Aufpasser, Fremde erschienen
Uns überdeutlich wie diejenigen, die uns brauchen könnten

Auch unsere Wälder, die Lianen, den Boden. Tage dümpelten
Im Röhricht, wir sahen die Sonne sinken, sahen Palmkronen

Und blitzende Makrelen im Wasser, die neben den Booten
Im Lichtschein der Fackeln schwärmten, zählten die sanften

Nächte des wolkenlosen Mondes an zwei Händen, sammelten
Uns Beeren in den Mund, wir kannten das Wort Zufriedenheit

Noch nicht

1

Low, wired-like walls, nibbled-on green
Long, nondescript buildings, could be barracks

Or dog breeding on a grand scale, we in turn
Thought animals multiplied on their own, needed

Neither dog breeders nor watchdogs, strangers appeared
All too clearly to us like those who might have need of us

Also our forests, the lianas, the ground. Days bobbed up and down
In the reeds, we saw the sun sinking, saw tops of palm trees

And sparkling mackerels in the water which swarmed next to
The boats in the glare of the torches, counted the mellow

Nights with a cloudless moon on both hands, collected
Berries in our mouths, we didn't know the word satisfaction

Just yet

2

Wir lebten im Zwischenland zwischen zwei Flüssen, sahen
Das Meer, eine unerschöpfliche Nahrungsquelle im Grünlichen

Wir hatten sieben Worte für Regen, drei für Flut und keines
Das annähernd für „ich" stand. Wir sagten Bruder, Onkelkind

Wir hatten Namen, die uns genügten, wie Häute, Reuse, Fischgräte
Wir wußten nicht, daß wir „wild" waren, die Fremden nannten uns so

Wir hatten anmaßende Augen, mit denen sahen wir kein Unglück
Über uns kommen, der Kalender war noch nicht erfunden, die Uhr

Hieß Gezeitenmaß, die Fremden waren auch wild, wenn sie tranken
Schossen sie in die Luft, auf Haustiere, wir gingen ihnen aus dem Weg

Damit sie nicht auf uns schössen, wir lernten die Furcht kennen, „ich"
Sagen zu müssen (Fremdsprache): „Ich habe Angst, verstehe nichts.

Wirklich."

2

We lived on the land between the two rivers, saw
The sea, an inexhaustible source of nourishment shimmering green

We had seven words for rain, three for flood and none
Which approximated "I." We said brother, uncle-child

We had names that sufficed, like skins, bow nets, fish bones
We didn't know that we were "uncivilized," the strangers called us that

We had insolent eyes, with them we saw no misfortune
Come over us, the calendar was not yet invented, the clock

Was called tidal scale, the strangers were also uncivilized when they drank
They shot in the air, at house pets, we kept out of their way

So that they didn't shoot at us, we became acquainted with the fear of
Having to say "I" (foreign language): "I am afraid, understand nothing.

                                            Really."

3

Noch einmal: Wo sind wir? Das Logbuch deutlicher als Verträge
Wir waren da, wo nichts war, unkartiert lebte unser Stamm, dürftig

Waren wir im Bodenlosen und im Sumpf des Flußufers, aufgerichtete
Vierbeiner, hörten Baumsägen kreischen, und Finken flatterten davon

Mit den Vögeln lebten wir nicht wie mit den Bäumen, aber die Vögel
Waren Wegweiser: wo keine Bäume, keine Vögel, kein Gekreisch

Letztlich auch wir nicht: Wo wir nicht waren, war alles, Blätterhaufen
Die wir beseelten ohne Muscheln und Verträge: wir warteten einfach

Daß die Seelen, die uns überlassen, atmeten, und wir wurden leise
Vor unserem inneren Auge, das brach und wieder auferstand, Ahnen

Sprachen nicht zu uns, wie wir es erhofften, letztlich also warfen wir
Hölzchen, rauchten, schwiegen, wußten nichts. Wie die Eroberer.

3

Once again: Where are we? The logbook more precise than contracts
We were there where there was nothing, our tribe lived unmapped, wretchedly

Were we in an abyss and in the marsh of the riverbank, four-legged creatures
Standing upright, heard pruning saws screeching, and finches fluttered away

With the birds we didn't live the same as with the trees, but the birds
Were guideposts: where there were no trees, no birds, no shrieking

Ultimately not us either: Where we were not, everything else was, leaf piles
That we brought to life without shells or contracts: we simply waited

For the souls surrendered to us to breathe, and we became quiet
Before our inner eye which broke and was resurrected, ancestors

Did not speak to us like we had hoped, so ultimately we threw
Bits of wood, smoked, were silent, knew nothing. Like the conquerors.

4

Die Fremden waren mit einem Helikopter gekommen, steckten
Röhren in unsere Erde, schien, als wollten sie dem Boden lauschen

Der stumm war, das wußten wir selbst, ihre Apparate vibrierten
Satellitenschüsseln wie Elefantenohren, in die sie Stille schaufelten

Die dann dröhnte, röhrte, Sträucher, Dickicht, der Wald verstummte
So viele Vögel, Federbällchen, die von Zweigen fielen ohne Ton

Sie bauten Schächte und gossen sie aus mit kaltem Beton, wir
Sahen ihnen zu, den Missionaren des Schürfens, wozu im Boden

Rühren, wenn alles offenbar, die Luft, die Mangroven, Vogeltod
Die Getränke, die sie mit einem Zischen oder Ploppen öffneten –

Sie waren mit Helikoptern gekommen, um uns zu beeindrucken
Aber wir waren nicht beeindruckt, vielleicht aus Unerfahrenheit.

4

The strangers had come by means of a helicopter, inserted pipes
Into our earth, appeared as if they wanted to listen to the ground

Which was mute, we knew that ourselves, their devices vibrated
Satellite dishes like elephant ears into which they shoveled silence

Which then droned, roared, bushes, thicket, the forest was hushed
So many birds, little fluff balls which fell from branches without a sound

They built shafts and filled them with cold cement, we
Watched them, the missionaries of digging, why stir up

The ground if all apparent, the air, the mangroves, bird death
The beverages they opened with a fizzing or popping –

They had come by helicopter in order to impress us
But we were not impressed, perhaps out of inexperience.

5

Wir teilten die Fische und die Beute, verzögerten die Ankunft
Der Flut, indem wir Dämme bauten aus Reisig und Sand, das

Genügte, wir waren Wächter, weil wir nichts anderes kannten
Wir kannten Tiere und Pflanzen, die brechenden Äste im Sturm

Regen war ein Vorhang, wir spürten den feuchten Sand, den
Wir uns in die Sohlen rieben, der im Haar klebte bei Springflut

Wir holten Holz und verbrannten es, Holz war da wie Nichtich
Und während das eine verbrannte, war Nichtich biegsam wie

Gräten oder künstliches Material, Vinyl, Discjockeys, Halbvokale
Eine Wörterflut, so überflüssig wie ein Kropf, die wir redlich

Ach, was sag ich, und wer bin ich, die wir redlich teilten und
Was danach blieb, als wir uns schlafen gelegt hatten bei Vollmond

                              Nahmen die Fremden.

5

We divided up the fish and the loot, delayed the arrival
Of the flood by building dams out of sticks and sand, which

Sufficed, we were watchmen because we knew no differently
We knew animals and plants, the breaking boughs in the storm

Rain was a curtain, we felt the damp sand which we rubbed
Into our soles, which got stuck in our hair at springtide

We fetched wood and burned it, wood was there like not-I
And while the one was being burned, not-I was supple like

Fish bones or synthetic material, vinyl, disc jockeys, semivowels
A flood of words, as superfluous as a craw, which we fairly

Oh, what am I saying, and who am I, which we fairly divided up and
What was left over, when we had lain down to sleep at the full moon

                                        The strangers took.

6

„Vor drei Jahrhunderten kamen sie wegen Sandelholz, nun
Wollen sie unsere Gene, wollen uns ganz und gar!" Fördern

Scharfe Gewürze den Schweiß, fördert Hunger das Denken
Unter der Bedingung, daß Übergriffe sich nicht wiederholen?

Zimt oder Pfeffer, Garnelen, lange gilt die Unschuldsvermutung
So wie Gewürzverarbeitung, Stimulierung von Gefühlen, alles

Um eine Wirkung zu erzeugen, die uns strikt beschämen mußte
Wir wußten nur, wie wehrlos wir waren, niemand griff an.

Wir lernten, daß Geld keine seriöse Sache ist und auch jäh –
Nach Vereinbarung funktioniert es oder nicht (Kaurimuscheln)

Banditen kamen und blieben, handelten mit Gewürzen, mit uns
Bis wir uns selbst als Banditen sahen in einer unmäßigen Zone.

6

"Three centuries ago they came on account of sandalwood, now
They want our genes, want us entirely!" Do pungent

Spices stimulate sweat, does hunger stimulate the thought
Process with the stipulation that invasions do not recur?

Cinnamon or pepper, shrimp, the presumption of innocence is valid
For a long time just like processing spices, stimulating senses, all

In order to create an effect that made us feel severely ashamed
We knew only how defenseless we were, no one attacked.

We learned that money is no respectable matter and unexpected too –
By agreement it either works or it doesn't (cowrie shells)

Bandits came and remained, trafficked in spices, in us
Until we saw ourselves as bandits in an intemperate zone.

7

Und wir gaben eine Handbreit nach und wollten nur etwas Stickstoff
Um unsere Felder zu düngen, wollten den kleinen Finger reichen

Versteckten den Daumen der rechten Hand, boten Früchte, Nüsse
Aber die andere Seite lachte, sie schickte Ingenieure, sie bohrte

Unseren Ahnen in den modernden Knochen und in Heiligtümern
Von Alters her; so geht das nicht, sagten unsere Ältesten, aber ein

Wedeln mit Verträgen weckte Wünsche, die wir ebenfalls hatten
Sie ließen unsere Palmblätterhütten abbrennen und setzten Baracken

Wo wir Windgesänge gehört. Was noch, fragten wir, haben wir nicht
Eigentum an unseren eigenen Leben und Matten und Trinkschalen

Und unsere Ältesten stießen mit den Köpfen zusammen, hielten Rat
Während unsere Tiere den Unrat plünderten, den die Fremden ließen.

7

And we retreated a hand's breadth and wanted only some nitrogen
To fertilize our fields, wanted to extend our little finger

Hid the thumbs of our right hands, offered fruits, nuts
But the other side laughed, they sent engineers, drilled

Into the rotting bones of our ancestors and into sanctuaries
From long ago; we can't allow that, said our elders, but

Dangling the carrot of a treaty aroused desires we had anyway
They had our palm leaf huts burned to the ground and built barracks

Where we heard wind songs. What else, we asked, don't we have
Ownership of our own lives and mats and drinking vessels

And our elders put their heads together, held council
While our animals rummaged through the refuse the strangers left.

8

Wortlose Zufriedenheit war ein Fell, das uns in kühlen Nächten
Umhüllte, die Fremden zogen es uns über den Kopf, verkauften

Es teurer als erwartet, nennenswerten Widerstand gab's nicht
In den Rankings des Weltmarkts traten wir nicht in Erscheinung

So waren wir, tumbe Leute im windgepeitschten Hinterwald
Galten als freundschaftlich übertölpelbar, Glasperlen und Dünger

Letztlich begriffen wir selbst nicht, was Zufriedenheit war ohne
Ein Wort, ohne Gewißheit der niedergebrannten Glut, Holzasche

Ließ uns kalt, nicht aber Trommeln in klaren Nächten, uns schwitzte
Das Brusthaar am Hauptfesttag des lebendigen Lebens, Arschoffen

(So nannten wir ihn). Wir spürten, was fehlte, ein eisiger Hauch, aber
Wortlos, der Mond bremste die Sorge um den Fehler, der nicht wirklich

Ein Fehler war: Wolkenlosigkeit

8

Wordless satisfaction was a woolen blanket that covered us on cool
Nights, the strangers pulled the wool over our heads, sold it for more

Than expected, resistance worth mentioning didn't exist
In the rankings of the global market we did not appear

That's how we were, dummies in the wind-whipped backwoods
Considered amicably gullible, glass beads and fertilizer

Ultimately we didn't comprehend what satisfaction was without
A word, without certainty of the burned-down blaze, wood ash

Left us cold, but not drums on clear nights, our chest hair
Sweated on the main feast day of this lively life, Bare-Ass

(As we called it). We sensed what was missing, an icy breath, but
Wordless, the moon curbed worries about the mistake that really wasn't

A mistake: Cloudlessness

9

Daß wir ein Rohstoff geworden waren, leuchtete uns ein, ein Beben
Daß wir eine Wunde waren, in die Salz hineingestreut werden konnte

Wissen hieß: gewesenes Wissen, tote Fische, Wissen über Fisch=
Ströme und Wasserstraßen, die die Fische zogen und wir ihnen nach

Dafür gab es keine Sprache oder eine aus Fischmehl, Palmwein
Abstoßend, die Fremden verweisend, gab es jemals die Vermischung

Die die Rohstoffe untermischt wie Plankton, Seeigelgekröse wie
Frauen, die in die Städte gehen und sich leidlich verkaufen, gab es

In den Ärschen der Kinder eine Wunde, die „vielleicht" hieß oder „ja"
Oder „nie und nimmer": Wenn du mich mitnimmst weit weg von hier?

Gab es das, gab es die Fremden mit den Leitungen und Bohrungen
Gab es uns, ins Schauen gebannt, in Wirklichkeit undurchschaubar?

9

It dawned on us that we had become a commodity, an inkling
That we were a wound into which salt could be rubbed

Knowledge meant: former knowledge, dead fish, knowledge of fish –
Streams and waterways that the fish traveled and we after them

For that there was no language or one made of fish meal, palm wine
Repulsive, rebuking the strangers, was there ever the commingling

Which mixed up the resources like plankton, sea urchin mesentery like
Women who go to the cities and sell themselves poorly, was there

A wound in the asses of children called "perhaps" or "yes"
Or "never ever": If you take me along far away from here?

Did that exist, did the strangers exist with the pipelines and drill holes
Did we exist, spellbound into looking, in reality impenetrable?

10

„Vielleicht" oder „ja" war kein Argument für die Fischschwärme
Ihr *Cruisen* auf alten Routen, in Wellensäumen, aber die Fremden

Die kamen, wußten, wer wir waren, und wir glaubten ihnen nicht
Wir waren die Früheren, Stehengebliebenen, wir waren glücklich

Wenn wir die Muschel rieben, während die Fremden ihr Telefon
Ans Ohr preßten, verbunden mit Gott und der Welt, während sie

Mit uns scherzten im T-Shirt und in Khaki-Shorts, rotbeinig verbrannt
Die Nasen mehrfach gehäutet, hatten wir es mit den Garnelen zu tun

Und Booten im Hafen und den Verträgen im Hotel und Dolmetschern
Die uns wohlweislich nicht verstehen, wir aber doch: Hitzedesaster

Vogelsterben. Wo ist das, was einmal war und was wir waren ohne
Ein Wort wie Geschichte, aber pfeilgerade gesetzt wie ein Schmerz?

10

"Perhaps" or "yes" was not an argument for the shoals of fish
Their cruising on old routes, on the wavy edges, but the strangers

Who came knew who we were and we didn't believe them
We were the earlier ones, those left standing, we were happy

When we ground shells while the strangers held their telephones
To their ears, connected to everyone under the sun, while they

Joked with us in T-shirts and khaki shorts, sunburned legs red
Their noses peeling repeatedly, we were busy with the shrimp

And boats in the harbor and the contracts in the hotel and interpreters
Who wisely don't understand us, but we do them: heat disaster

Birds dying. Where is that which once was and which we were without
A word like history, but set straight as an arrow like sorrow?

11

Die Fremden gaben uns Satellitentelefone in großen Säcken, doch
Mit wem sollten wir telefonieren, wenn sie in den Boden bohrten

Waren unsere Telefone tot, so schien es uns, aber bewiesen waren
Nur die Verträge, bündeldick, die sie uns gaben, die wir nicht lasen

Wir lasen in ihren Körpern, im Rotgesichtigen, im Sandalentragen
Das ihre Füße quälte, sie sahen nicht gesund aus, und wir starrten

Den Fischschwärmen nach, die ausblieben, seit Fremde gekommen
Aber wir kamen und gingen nicht, anders als die Wellen, die kamen

Und nahmen. Die Zentralregierung döste in einem langen Schlaf
Auf Löschblättern und Palmwedeln, von Bezirksfürsten gewiegt

Wir tippten die Nummern ein, hinter denen Abwesenheit bis ins
Letzte Glied, so wurden wir ruhig, ruhiggestellt und die Leitung

Blieb Scheintot.

11

The strangers gave us satellite telephones in big sacks, yet
Whom should we call, when they drilled in the ground

Our telephone lines went dead, so it seemed to us, but the only proof
Was the contracts they gave us which we didn't read, thickly packaged

We read into their bodies, the red-facedness, the sandal-wearing
That bothered their feet, they didn't look healthy, and we stared

Past the shoals of fish that had not appeared since the strangers came
But we did not come and go, different from the waves that came

And took away. The central government dozed in a long sleep
Swayed by district lords, we typed numbers on blotting paper

And palm fronds, behind which absence up to the last limb
Thus we became immobile, immobilized and the phone line

                    Was apparently still dead.

12

Wir ließen zu, daß sie den Boden aufrührten Kiesel spritzten
Wir sahen zu, wie sie Frauen betatschten, die stöhnten, daß

Es keine Art, wohlig oder nicht, wir wollten das nicht wissen
Und schließlich betatschten wir uns selbst, Schenkel, das Glied

Stöhnten, als wären wir befriedigt, wir kannten Wörter wie
„Zufriedenheit" endlich, Wind kühlte unsere heißen Hoden, aber

Die Frauen waren den Fremden im Nu zu alt, der Boden aufgewühlt
Die Ebene zwischen der Küste und den Flüssen, wir standen auf

Unseren eigenen Füßen, nichts war wirklich geschehen, Süßwasser
Mischte sich mit salzigem der Bucht, der Wind zärtelte an Knospen

Wir lernten die Sprache der Invasoren, die ein Hüftschwung war
Über streng verteilten Katasterbescheiden, die ins Wasser fielen.

12

We allowed them to stir up the ground, gravel sprayed
We watched as they groped women who groaned, that

It was no way to act, pleasurable or not, we didn't want to know that
And ultimately we groped ourselves, thighs, our members

Groaned as if we were gratified, we finally knew words like
"Satisfaction," wind cooled our hot testicles, but the women

Were at once too old for the strangers, the ground torn up
The plain between the coast and the rivers, we stood upon

Our own two feet, nothing had really happened, freshwater
Mixed with saltwater from the bay, the wind caressed buds

We learned the language of the invaders as a hip swing
Above strictly dispensed cadastral decisions which failed.

X

Koalition

so geisterhaft sind diese späten Tage

X

Coalition

so spooky these late days are

1

Natürlich traten die üblichen Vermittler auf, aber sie hatten
Keine Blicke, weil alles gesagt war und unser Tagungsthema

Mit allerhöchster Unterstützung auf den runden Tisch gelegt
So störte niemand, nur die Sache stand starr im Raum und war

Nicht wirklich greifbar. (Sehr weit hätte es eine Veranstaltung
Gebracht.) Bringschuld: Wird die Konferenz ein Erfolg? Anderes

Undenkbar und wie es weitergeht unleugbar mit Sachen verknüpft
Von Wissenschaft und mit hoher Wahrscheinlichkeit wie bisher

Brachen die üblichen Vermittler ihre Bahn: Rodung & Anpflanzung
Appelle perlten an den vollendeten Manieren der Teilnehmer ab

Eine Hand wäscht den Staub als Äquivalent der Enttäuschung ab
Jemand sagt: „Versöhnlichkeit ist eine persönliche Entscheidung."

1

Of course the customary mediators appeared, but they had
No views since all had been said and our meeting topic

Was brought to the round table with the highest endorsement by everyone
So no one interrupted, only the matter stayed fixed in the room and was

Not really comprehensible. (A presentation would have meant a great
Deal.) Debt to be paid: Will the conference be a success? Otherwise

Unthinkable and how it proceeds undeniably linked to matters
Of science and as always in great probability

The customary mediators paved the way: clearing & sowing
Appeals slid off the perfected manners of the participants

A hand washes off the dust as the equivalent to disappointment
Someone says: "Conciliatoriness is a personal decision."

2

Auch unser Tagungsthema verlangt von den Opfern Vergebung
Etwas in Gang Gebrachtes fliegt auf, etwas in Gängen und Fluren

Gemunkeltes, wenn wir die gesundheitlichen Nachteile, Narben
Und Amputationen in Rechnung stellen – wie langsam vorgehen

Wie langsam zurück, jetzt möchten wir dauerhaft Gesichertes
Hilflosigkeit dringt in den Raum, Überforderung und Erschöpfung

Der Helfer, die etwas in Gang noch lange nicht zu Ende gebracht
Schweigen aus Überforderung, Schweigen füllt den öden Raum

Versuche, Frauen in die Klinik zu bringen, Bettlerinnen und
Prostituierte, das Schweigen überwältigend wie Sprachhürden

Heißt: Erweiterung der Geschichte, Ausbeulung, Spätgeräusche
Und was, wenn die Programme zu Ende? Lichtwechsel, Regen.

2

Our meeting topic also requires forgiveness from the victims
Something set in motion takes flight, something in halls and corridors

Things rumored, when we take the health risks, scars
And amputations into account – like proceeding slowly

Thus returning slowly, now we would like things permanently guaranteed
Helplessness permeates the room, excessive demands and exhaustion

Of the aides who have not set anything in motion for a long time now
Silence due to excessive demands, silence fills the desolate room

Attempts to bring women to the clinic, beggar women and
Prostitutes, the silence overpowering like language barriers

Means: expanding history, bulging out, late noises
And what, when the programs over? Change of light, rain.

3

Wenn wir uns auf die Seite des Ich schlagen, bricht der Boden
Wenn wir uns nicht auf die Seite des Ich stellen, zerbrechen wir

Bliebe noch, sich auf die Seite des Rätsels zu schlagen, wir sind ja
Geschlagen im grandios Hellhörigen mit überlappenden Wendungen

Wenn wir annehmen, hier sei nichts, nur kalter Atem, der einschließt
Ausgehauchte Moleküle, Geräuschempfinden und Zerstörung

Wenn wir das methodische Angreifen aufgreifen, geschlagen mit
Heillosem Denken, sich verschränkenden Figuren, kopflos sind wir

Noch nicht, wenn wir annehmen Fingernägel und Sternschnuppen
All das Gelichter und das Aufblitzen von Schönheit sei unbedacht

Wenn wir denken, daß wir nicht denken ins Unmögliche nur
Beiläufig gekrümmt. Genaueres hat man noch nicht gewußt.

3

When we cast our lots with the ego, the ground cracks
When we do not align ourselves with the ego, we snap

What remains is casting our lots with the mystery, we are surely
Defeated in the grandiose clairaudience with overlapping turns

When we assume nothing is here, only cold breath that includes
Exhaled molecules, sense of sound and destruction

When we seize upon the methodical attack, defeated by
Unholy thinking, interlocking figures, we are not yet

Headless, when we assume fingernails and shooting stars
All the riffraff and the flickering of beauty would be rash

When we think that we are not thinking of the impossible only
Randomly crooked. More precise details were not yet known.

4

Waisen wachsen auf, gewaltsamer Verlust, wissen nichts mehr
Von den Höhlen, dem rußigen Herd, dem sie entwuchsen

In einem rapiden Prozeß, Deterritorialisierung, Stimmverlust
Gleichmütig hingenommen, wie Wasser in flachen Pfützen steht

Gewehre und Cholera, Esel am artesischen Brunnen, Blutfluß
Waisen irren umher, schniefend, wir fangen sie ein wie Wildpferde

Traumatischer Augenblick für Helfer und Handelsdelegationen
Reisschalen und Hirsefladen, Ernährung und Erziehungsziele

Weiche Themen in beinharter Zeit, während die Hüftschaufeln
Der unbillig Hingeschiedenen, flüchtig verscharrt, zerfallen

Tiere schleichen sich an, Kindersoldaten ohne Auftrag wissen
Warum und wer sie füttert, Waisen wollen bei uns nicht bleiben.

4

Orphans grow up, oppressive damage, know nothing more
About the caves, the sooty stove that they outgrew

In a rapid process, deterritorialization, aphonia
Serenely accepted, like water stands in flat puddles

Guns and cholera, donkeys at the artesian fountain, flow of blood
Orphans wander about, sniffling, we rope them in like wild horses

Traumatic moment for aides and trade delegations
Rice bowls and millet cakes, nourishment and nurturing

Bland topics for a tough-as-nails time, while the hip sockets
Of the unfairly deceased, hastily buried, are decomposing

Animals sneak up, child soldiers without authority know
Why and who feeds them, orphans do not want to stay with us.

5

Wichtig ist es, einen runden Tisch geschickt zu bestücken
Das große politische Stühlerücken, wer neben wem wann

Und welche Maßnahmen unter den gestreiften Markisen
Protokoll heißt der Weg übers Eis, das Kolonnen tragen muß

Ein Rattenschwanz von Verordnungen, um das Ende zu besiegeln
Besichtigung der unzerstörten Hügel, ein gelassenes Kommuniqué

Was zerstört wurde, bleibt nicht, wir gewähren leichte Kredite
Und wichtig sind die kleinen Schritte, Hirse und Kürbis, Ziegel

Nägel, um zwei Latten aufeinander zu kloppen, Ruhigstellung
Der niedergeworfenen Gegner durch Ausgangssperre, Kontrolle

Die Hand, die ausgestreckt, ist nicht leer, Panzer patrouillieren
Und die Betonpiste des Flughafens ist eine friedliche Ebene

5

It is important to skillfully assemble a round table
The great political musical chairs, who next to whom when

And which measures beneath the striped marquees
Protocol means the way over the ice which must withstand convoys

A whole string of regulations in order to seal the end
Visit to the undestroyed hills, a placid communiqué

What was destroyed does not remain, we grant easy credit
And important are the small steps, millet and pumpkin, bricks

Nails to batten two slats on top of each other, immobilization
Of the prostrated enemy by means of curfew, surveillance

The hand extended is not empty, tanks are patrolling
And the concrete runway of the airport is a peaceful plateau

6

Stockholmsyndrom angeglichen: auch ich wollte ein Komet
Sein, wollte still und rein, gleißend weit weg, weggeschlossen

Also: sich versteifend ausgeliefert an eine Hand, die eine
Muskelsprache spricht, nackte Fingernägelbefehle, Sehnen

Nach galaktischen Räumen & war ein Kind, das wollte nie
War ein Komet, der rollte. Opfer waren in Gefangenschaft

Ganz unterwürfig, maullappig, sich schurgelnd an der Feind=
Materie, die nicht überraschend die Gesichtsmaske aufbehielt

Enttäuschende Entwicklung, auch täuschend ähnlich mit mir
Selbstmission beendet: „kometenhafter Aufstieg". Abwurf.

Verhandlungstaktik zwischen Sprechen und Zuhören, Schein=
Dialog. Taten Fremden Gewalt an, schmerzte uns nicht einmal.

6

Stockholm syndrome approximated: even I wanted to be a comet
Wanted to be still and pure, blazing far away, locked up

So: stiffly at the mercy of a hand that speaks
A language of muscles, bare fingernail orders, longing

For galactic spaces & was a child that never wanted
Was a comet that rolled. Victims were in captivity

Fully submissive, flabby mouthed, bullying themselves about the
Adversarial material, not surprisingly keeping their face masks on

Disappointing development, also deceptively similar to me
Mission of one completed: "meteoric ascent." Release.

Negotiating strategy between speaking and listening, pseudo –
Dialog. Did violence to strangers, didn't even hurt ourselves.

7

Als ob sich das Universum an diesem einen Ort verdichtete
Mit Druck aus sich herauszupressen die Ereignisse wie

Eine Ballung von Energie, Weltentwurf, verworfene Idee
Zudem sind alle Wörter eingeladen, aufgeladen, beladen

Zunder, Sonntagsgefühl, Tagungsteilnehmer erfinden sich
Den historischen Augenblick: Schulterschluß Mundverschluß

Gesättigte Mehrfachbewerber kramen ihre Verdienstorden aus
Wohin denn, wenn nicht zurück zum Ausschweif stundenlang

Beratung, wo jetzt Bestrahlung eines strittigen Deutungspotentials
Werfen sich Bälle zu, fallen gelassene Überzeugungen, taktisch

Auch faktisch Ziehn im Kreuz, hauruck und vorsorgliche Verträge
Mit erfahrenen Fachleuten, daß allerorten gefälligst Konsens entsteht

7

As if the universe became condensed at this one place
With pressure to squeeze out of itself events like

An agglomeration of energy, world concept, discarded idea
Furthermore all words are uploaded, loaded, laden

Tinder, Sunday feeling, meeting participants invent
The historic moment: shoulder to shoulder mouth closure

Satiated multiple applicants display their service medals
Where to then, if not back to the excess for hours on end

Consultation where now exposure to a disputed capacity to interpret
Throw balls to each other, convictions abandoned, tactically

Also actually pulling in the back, heave ho and preventive contracts
With experienced specialists so that consensus had better arise everywhere

8

Wenn allerorten Konsens entsteht, zerbröselt zwischen Baum und
Borke gewachsene Kompetenz. Ein Machen und Tun, Verhandlung

Tief in die Wasseradernacht. Schultern werden geklopft, daß Staub
Aufwirbelt. Wie Blüten aufbrechen am frühen Morgen und welken

Alles in die Hand der Verhandlungspartner gelegt, Stäbe, welche
Tagen bis in die späte Nacht und werden gebrochen über Gräbern

Verschlossene Türen und Mikrophone im Schalltoten. Dann Hell=
Hörigkeit wie Gewitter, Bleivergossenheit, Meinungsverdrossenheit

Glänzte mit Nahkampferfahrung, und Gott ruhte am siebten Tag
Durchgearbeitet wurde zugunsten des Ergebnisses. Koalition aus Regen

Und Nichtregen, Graupeln, Hagel sowie Schirmen, gut durchdacht
Verstärkt von weitsichtigen Emissären, die sich in trockene Tücher

8

When consensus arises everywhere, grown competence crumbles
Between a rock and a hard place. Much ado and to do, negotiation

Deep into the water vein night. Backs are being patted so that dust
Swirls up. Like blossoms open in the early morning and wither

All laid into the hands of the negotiating partners, staffs which
Meet until late into the night and are broken over graves

Locked doors and microphones in soundproofing. Then clair –
Audience like thunderstorms, moldings of lead, dolefulness of opinion

Excelled in hand-to-hand combat experience and God rested on the seventh day
Was worked through for the benefit of the result. Coalition made of rain

And non-rain, sleet, hail as well as umbrellas, well thought through
Intensified by farsighted emissaries safely tucked away in dry cloths

9

Die Tücher waren so trocken nicht, bildlich gesprochen flatterten sie
Man sah sie im Wind, gegenständlich flattern, Sturm kam auf, blieb

Tücher wie Bücher, die man aufschlug, um Rat bat, der blieb aus
Aufschlagen, aufkeimen, auf der Lauer liegen, Tücher zum Bleichen

In zertrennter Luft, sinket am tiefsten zu Boden. Und wenn man
Gefangen wäre in der Karosserie, gefesselt am Steuer vom Sitzgurt

Die Wörter wie Wild aufgescheucht, kopflos ins Lauffeuer
Liefen, und es war selbstverständlich, daß sie benutzt, vernutzt –

Alle Wörter, alle Wörter, ein Halali der Wörter, zur Strecke gebracht
Vor der langen Nacht, wer sich in die Büsche geschlagen, lachte nie

Später las man vom „Behagen, am Leben zu sein", und die Stimme
Die es aussprach, zitterte nicht, zwar gab es die Probe aufs Exempel

9

The cloths were not so dry, figuratively speaking they were fluttering
One saw them in the wind, graphically fluttering, storm came up, stayed

Cloths like books one flipped open, asked for advice that was not given
Flipping open, bursting forth, lying in wait, cloths for bleaching

In disrupted air, would sink most deeply to the ground. And if one
Were trapped inside the car, bound at the wheel by the seat belt

The words scared off like deer, ran headless into the wild
Fire, and it was self-evident that they were used, misused –

All words, all words, a death halloo of words, hunted down
Before the long night, whoever driven into the bushes never laughed

Later one read about the "pleasure of being alive," and the voice
That spoke did not tremble, indeed the rule was put to the test

10

„Als wir anfingen, uns vorurteilsvoll zu begegnen, halfen wir uns
Mit einem gedanklichen Kartenspiel, ausgeben, aufeinanderlegen

Übertrumpfen turmhoch." Gedanke schlägt Stuhl, Stuhl schlägt
Tischbein, Tischbein schlägt Wade undsoweiter. Beglaubigte

Abschriften. Wo gehobelt wird, fliegen. Vögel nicht. (Auslassung)
Als solche feindl. empfunden: das sind doch nur Bruchstücke, die.

Und waren der Begründungen verlustig gegangen, lausig, waren
Schnürgesenkelt ungelenk. Dann aber mit abgründigen Sonnenbrillen

Verbündet aufgebockt, Wasserkanister, Container, Brunnenbauer
Wadenbeißer. Statthalter. In der Gunst der Stunde entsteht alles neu

Kompromittiert sich nicht: „aber bißchen dalli, wenn ich bitten darf".
Menschenwürde. Menschenfleisch. Menschenskind. Hansaplast.

10

"When we began to encounter ourselves with prejudice, we helped ourselves
With a mental card game, dealing, playing cards one on top of the other

Trumping sky-high." Thought beats chair, chair beats
Table leg, table leg beats calf and so on. Certified

Transcripts. Where there's smoke, flying. Not birds. (Omission)
As such perceived as antag.: those are simply fragments which.

And had forfeited the foundations, shoddily, were
Clumsily shoelaced. But then jacked up, allied with

Inscrutable sunglasses, water canisters, containers, well diggers
Heel nippers. Governors. By seizing the day everything begins anew

Does not compromise itself: "but make it snappy, if you please."
Human dignity. Human flesh. Man alive. Band-Aid.

11

Ein Wort wurde nach unserem Sieg grundsätzlich geächtet
Wo es gestanden hatte, wurde es geschwärzt und gelyncht

Es hieß „Feind" und wo Feind war, waren wir nicht willkommen
Wo wir waren, wollten wir geachtet sein, und was ist eine Frau

Die sich heimlich hinter ihrem Ohrgehänge die Haut aufkratzt
Keine niedergeschlagenen Augen, eher Neugierblitze wie eine

Gebeugt über einen Zuber, in dem sie geblümte Wäsche wringt
Wäre das Wort „Feindberührung" nicht getilgt, wären wir lässiger

Beamte des *Foreign Office* veröffentlichen Instruktionen, Datteln
Pflücken ist verboten, und die Minensuchtrupps säubern Parks

Ruinenlandschaftsverband, Geäst, Rodung, Empfindungslosigkeit.
Vorwärtsverteidigung war ein Losungswort nach unsrem Geschmack

11

One word was categorically outlawed after our victory
Wherever it had been, it was blackened and lynched

It was called "foe" and wherever foe was, we were not welcome
Wherever we were, we wanted to be respected, and what is a woman

Who secretly scratches open the skin behind dangly earrings
No lowered eyes, rather flashes of curiosity like one

Bent over a tub in which she is wringing out flowery laundry
If the words "contact with the enemy" weren't erased, we'd be more casual

Civil servants of the Foreign Office publish briefings, picking
Dates is forbidden and mine-seeking troops clean up parks

Society for ruined landscapes, branches, clearing, anesthesia.
Forward defense was a password according to our taste

12

Andere wiederum beneiden den Brunnenbauer, den Grabschaufler
Durch Erdschichten, Lehm, Schotter, Gestein der Erdwärme zu

Glühendes Magma, das schlußendl. auch den planenden Verstand
Versengt. Gedanken gibt es, die man ganz schnell denken muß

Dächte man sie langsam, käme man zu anderen Ergebnissen
Verzweiflungszetern – ob das Denken geholfen, ist nicht sicher

Der Sand war so tief, Erdflocken stoben auf und spritzten
Auf das Ölzeug des Brunnenbauers, über den Schlacht gelehnt

Andere wiederum mit regennassen Segeln aufgetakelt oder
Enden als Bungeespringer an Küsten und Brückengeländern

In ihren Gesichtern und Gebärden keinerlei Freude, ähnlich
Hochlandbewohnern, Häuslern, die herkommen, als gäbe es

Was geschenkt.

12

Others in turn envy the well digger, the grave shoveller
Through layers of earth, loam, gravel, rocks of terrestrial heat into

Glowing magma that ultimat. also singes the scheming
Mind. There are thoughts that must be quickly thought

If they were slowly thought, different conclusions would arise
Clamoring of despair – whether thinking helped is not certain

The sand was so deep, flakes of earth flew up and sprayed
The oilskins of the well digger, leaning over the shaft

Others in turn rigged with rain-wet sails or
End up as bungee jumpers on coasts and balustrades

In their faces and gestures no joy whatsoever, similar to
Highlanders, cottagers who come here as if there were

                              Something for free.

XI

Selbststimulation

Philoktet in zwölf humpelnden Schritten

XI

Self-stimulation

Philoctetes in twelve hobbling steps

1

Dies ist mein Fuß, dies ist der pochende Schmerz, hier
Schleppt sich fort, was nicht zu ertragen, schleppe mich
Selbst, schleppe das schmerzende Bein als eine Eisenlast
Schleppe ich eine Sträflingskugel und die eitrige Binde
Die den Fuß bedeckt, eine lange Leine, die an den Krieg
Mich knüpft, gefesselt bin ich ans holprige Gehen und
Staksen, und was aus der Wunde rinnt, schwärender Rotz:
Abstoßend bin ich mir selbst, Träger des Wundmals und
Eines eisernen Kreuzes, das, auf die Wunde gelegt, nicht
Den Wundbrand verhindert hat. Abstoßend ist mein Fuß
Wollte ihn selbst abstoßen in einem Sommerschlußverkauf
Könnte ich ihn loswerden um jeden Preis, aber er blieb mir

1

This is my foot, this is the throbbing pain, it drags
Itself along here, not to be endured, drag myself
On my own, drag the aching leg like an iron weight
I drag a ball and chain and the pus-filled bandage
That covers the foot, a long cord that links me
To the war, I am bound to clumsy walking and
Teetering, and flowing from the wound, festering snot:
I find myself disgusting, bearer of the stigma and
An iron cross, which, laid upon the wound, did not
Hinder the gangrene. My foot is disgusting
Wanted to cast it off myself in a summer sale
Would get rid of it at any price, but it remained

2

Erhalten habe ich eine Rente fürs Bein und für Erinnerung
Die schmerzt, es tropft der alte stinkige Eiter immer wieder
Aus frischem Wundverband, an den Kampf denk ich zurück
Gradlinig, in dem ein giftiger Pfeil, wie ihn im Köcher ich hatte
Mir den Fuß durchbohrte, mit gleicher Münze heimgezahlt
Der Sinn fürs Tragische ist eine blanke Scheidemünze, die aus
Dem Hosensack gezogen, Kopf oder Zahl, Gezähltes, das vergeht
Der Wundbrand frißt sich bis zum Knochen, Hinkebein schlurft
Durch eine verheerte Welt, daß eine Schlange mich gebissen hat
Daß kein Pfeil mich ritzte, als ich den Bogen trug, den Herakles
Mir gab: geschenkt, ich sperre die Information, ich will ein Opfer
Sein und nicht ein Waffenträger, den es erwischt, der ausgesetzt

2

I have received a pension for the leg and for memory
That hurts, the old stinking pus drips again and again
From fresh bandage, I think straight back to the battle
In which a poison arrow like the one I had in the quiver
Pierced my foot, giving me a taste of my own medicine
The sense of the tragic is a blank token coin pulled from
The pants pocket, heads or tails, countable things come to pass
The gangrene is eating through to the bone, gimpy leg shuffles
Through a ravaged world, that a snake has bitten me
That no arrow grazed me as I carried the bow that Heracles
Gave me: forget it, I block that information, I want to be a victim
And not a bearer of arms who gets nabbed, who is exposed

3

Auf einer Insel mit dem schwarzen Eiter und einem höllischen
Gestank, hätt ich eine Krücke, fragte man, was ist dir geschehn
Hast du dich vorgewagt als Meldegänger, als Patrouille?, nichts
Habe ich, hab die Waffen des Herakles getragen, bis sie schwer
Mir, ich habe Blut und Wasser geschwitzt und wollte heldisch
Sein wie alle und noch mehr, da war nichts mehr, die Insel brannte
In der Hitze, ich roch mich selbst, haßte meinen schlappen Fuß
Ernährte mich von Fischzeug, Tran und bitteren Kräutern, träufelte
Den Saft des Spitzwegerich in meine Wunde, es half nicht, ich trug
Den Kopf sehr hoch, sah auf das Meer, das schiffelos einsam war
Nun war ich abgeschnitten von der Gegenwart, glorreich die Waffen
An denen ich mich verhoben, vergessen die alte Welt, mir gewogen

3

On an island with the black pus and a hellacious
Stench, if I had a crutch, someone asked, what happened to you
Did you dare to advance as a harbinger, as patrol?, nothing
Did I dare, carried the weapons of Heracles until they were heavy
For me, I sweat blood and water and wanted to be heroic
Like all and even more, there was nothing more, the island burned
In the heat, I smelled myself, hated my limping foot
Nourished myself on fish stuff, blubber and bitter herbs, dripped
The juice of buckthorn onto my wound, it didn't help, I held
My head very high, saw the ocean which was shiplessly lonesome
Now I was cut off from the present, magnificent the weapons
I hurt myself lifting, the old world forgotten, favorable to me

4

Nichts half, ich half mir selbst nicht und keine Macht des Himmels
Anzurufen, der Sonne ausgesetzt, nutzlos und ausgesteuert als ein
Kriegsfossil, ein rostiger Panzer, Flugzeugträger eingemottet, noch
Nicht verschrottet, gut wäre es, ich verschrottete mich selbst und nur
Das Kampf-Gen, die Kampfhundmentalität überlebte als ein Klon
Von Philoktet, und wenn ich Fische briet und auf den Gräten kaute
Dachte ich ans Mannsbild, das ich einmal war, Maschine funktionierte
Die jetzt lahmgelegt, der heiße Ofen, der angespitzte Pfeil, gerichtet
Im Truppenverband, und nun richtet mich der Gestank der Wunde und
Ich verkriech mich, weil mich niemand braucht, ausgestoßen aus dem
Gemeinschaftsleben, wie sie die Hölle nannten, als sie sie bevölkerten
In meinem eigenen Krieg war ich mein eigner Feind, begehre Freund

4

Nothing helped, I didn't help myself and no power in heaven
To call upon, exposed to the sun, useless and rejected like a
War relic, rusty armor, aircraft carriers mothballed, still
Not scrapped, it would be good if I scrapped myself and only
The combat gene, the combat dog mentality survived as a clone
Of Philoctetes, and when I fried fish and chewed on the bones
I thought of the fellow that I once was, machine functioned
Now paralyzed, the hot oven, the sharpened arrow, aimed
At the unit, and now the stench of the wound condemns me and
I crawl away because no one needs me, cast out from the life
Of the community, as they referred to hell when they inhabited it
In my own personal war I was my own foe, desire a friend

5

Zu sein zumindest einem Tier, wenn mich der schwarze Fuß verläßt
Man ihn beschneiden muß, noch bin ich Zweibein, bin ich Kreatur
Allein in einer Welt aus Schmerz eingezwängt, ich winsele, wie ich es
Nie gehört, bin ich wildgewordener Schmerz, der nicht zu zähmen und
Alle anderen Hinkenden, Schmerzverzerrten sind mir ferngerückt und
Wurscht, hätt ich ein Schwert noch, ich hackte ab den eigenen Fuß, die
Reine Existenz des Schmerzes knüllt die Vergangenheit des Kriegers
In ein Tuch, in das der Eiter tropft, und was die Kampfmaschine war
Ist Heulen, Zähneknirschen, Leid (Sonderentwicklung von Selbstmitleid)
Und hatte einmal die Illusion, ein Wesen wie die schöne Helena wäre
Mein, sah mich als einen Bewerber, der sich getäuscht, sich selbst genarrt
Die Wahrheit ist: ich hatte Flausen im Kopf, nicht ungefährliche Waffen

5

To be at least an animal if the black foot abandons me
If it needs to be cut off, now I am still a bipod, I am a creature
Wedged into a world of pain alone, I whimper like I've
Never heard before, am I crazed pain, not to be tamed and
All other hobblers contorted in pain are far from me and I don't
Give a damn, if I still had a sword, I'd chop off my own foot, the
Pure existence of the pain crumples the warrior's past
Into a cloth the pus drips into, and whatever the combat machine was
Is now howling, gnashing of teeth, woe (side development of self pity)
And had the illusion, a being like the beautiful Helen of Troy would be
Mine, saw myself as a suitor who deceived himself, mocked himself
The truth is: my head was full of nonsense, not an innocuous weapon

6

Man sagte mir, man braucht mich wieder, braucht den Bogen, Reserve=
Kraft, ich kann mich nützlich machen, und ein Befehl ist ein Befehl, dem
Ich gehorchen sollte. Liefere die Waffen aus. Hier bin ich wieder, reihe
Mich ein von neuem, ich bin ein ausgelegter Köder für Trojaner einmal
Mehr, die Wunde heilt vor meinen Augen ohne Arzt, rasch eine junge Haut
Weil mich das Kriegsgeschehen wieder bindet, ich brauch den Fuß, ich
Brauch den Mut, die Hitze, Pfeilgerichtetheit, ich brauch, daß man mich
Braucht, ich spür den Drang, ich bin zielgerichtet, bin ein Pfeil, gespitzt
Losgelassen, los in einer Reihe aufgerichtet nicht mehr allein auf Lemnos
Und o Wunder, die Wunde schmerzt nicht mehr, ich tausche mich gegen
Einen künftigen Tod des Feindes, den ich nicht seh, ich sehe neuen Anfang
Sehe die Belagerer von Troja verschwommen, ich sehe mich vereint mit mir

6

I was told I am needed again, the bow is needed, reserve
Strength, I can be useful, and a command is a command which
I ought to obey. Supply weapons. Here I am again, lining up
Anew, I am a decoy designed for Trojans one more time
The wound heals before my eyes with no doctor, quickly a new skin
Because the warfare ties me down again, I need the foot, I need
The courage, the heat, arrow-orientation, I need to be needed
I sense the urge, I am goal-oriented, am an arrow, pointedly
Set free, freely erected in a row no longer alone on Lemnos
And oh wonder, the wound no longer hurts, I exchange myself for
A future death of the foe whom I do not see, I see a new beginning
See the besiegers of Troy in a haze, I see me united with myself

7

Dem früheren und zukünftigen Helden, ich bin gewappnet, weil ich stank
Kampfeshund, Kampfmaschine, Gegenpol zum Heulen und Resignieren
Der Mann, der stillstand in der Sonne, der das Bein nachzog, der winselte
Ich war das nicht, Schwamm drüber, jetzt geht's weiter, und ich gebe weiter
Was ich erlebt, hab ich nicht erstrebt, den Niedergang, aus dem ein Neues
Wurde: geh wieder kämpfen, Philoktet, was hast du sonst gelernt? Der Himmel
Ist besternt, die Erde blutig, die Schultern breit und schwankend ist der Mut
Nichts weißt du außer einem Vorwärts und der Angst, wenn's dir nicht weit
Genug ging: der Wald gerodet, die Stirn gegen den Felsen, Aasgeier fraßen
Nicht deinen Fuß, doch beinah hättest du ihn hergeschenkt, dafür gibst du dich
Hin und weg. Du bist der Kampf, und du bist Nichtkampf gewesen, aus war es.
Du warst ausgeschieden, und das ist dir schlecht bekommen, jetzt geknebelt

7

For the former and future hero, I am armed because I stank
Combat dog, combat machine, antithesis to howling and resignation
The man who stood still in the sun, who dragged his leg, who whimpered
It wasn't I, sponge on top of it, now we are moving on, and I am passing on
What I experienced, didn't I strive, the demise, out of which a new thing
Arose: go fight again, Philoctetes, what else have you learned? The heavens
Are starry, the earth bloody, the shoulders broad and courage is wobbly
You know nothing except for an advance and the fear when it did not go
Far enough for you: the forest cleared, nose to the grindstone, vultures did
Not eat your foot, yet you nearly gave it away, instead you give yourself
Carried away. You are the battle and you were the non-battle, it was over.
You were disqualified, and that did not agree with you, now gagged

8

Hast du dich übernommen an der Seite von Achilles' Sohn, aus dem nichts
Wird ohne dich, und du brauchst ihn auf Gedeih und Verderben, dazwischen
Die vermaledeiten Waffen, Erinnerung und der Geruch des Kampfes, tödlich
Ein Schwert im Rücken, du drehst dich um, damit es nicht trifft. Dich nicht.
Wäre ich auf der Insel geblieben, erhitzt, kläglich, wer hätte sich erinnert
An die Sterblichkeit, den großen Bogen, den der Krieger spuckt und pißt
Solang er aufrecht steht, und wenn er fällt, das Bein schlapp nachschleift
Schildkrötengleich im Panzer jammervoll verreckt, wer sieht ihn denn, wenn
Nicht die Spur des Elends Schatten wirft, so komm ich wieder, werfe mich
In eine Schale, die auch ein neuer Panzer, in dem ich glänze, neue Waffen
Alte Schule, Heldensage, mein Hut, mein Stock, mein Regenschirm, hart
Ausgesessene Tragödie, die ich nicht mehr versteh, Blut verständlicher als

8

Have you undertaken too much alongside Achilles' son, who will become
Nothing without you, and you need him through thick and thin, in between
The confounded weapons, memory and the smell of battle, fatally
A sword in the back, you turn around so that it doesn't strike. Not you.
If I had stayed on the island, heated up, pitiful, who would have recalled
The mortality, the great bow that the warrior spits and pisses on
As long as he stands upright, and when he falls, drags the leg limply behind
Like a tortoise perishing wretchedly in armor, who sees him then, when
Not a trace of misery casts shadows, so I will come again, throw myself
Into a hull that is also new armor in which I am radiant, new weapons
Old school, heroic saga, my hat, my cane, my umbrella, grimly sitting out
The tragedy I no longer understand, blood more comprehensible than

9

Ein Mensch, der sich und anderen etwas angetan. Ich möchte dumm sein
Und sehr seicht, ich denke mir es kinderleicht, achte mich nicht gering
Doch da ist die Perspektive: Geh und geh und kämpf und wirf wie früher
Eine Kampfmaschine an, bleib dran im besten Licht im Einvernehmen
Mit einer kalten Zukunft, die auf dem Tisch, man stirbt nicht an der Zukunft
Man stirbt an Ungelassenheit, der Fähigkeit, den Kopf zu verlieren, wenn
Er gebraucht, man stirbt nicht an einem kranken Fuß, an Dickköpfigkeit
Vielleicht, man stirbt an Sterbenstraurigkeit, die fällt, die fällt niemals
Voraussehbar. So muß Philoktet aufrecht stehen, warten, ob er fällt, wenn
Man ihn braucht, man braucht ihn, braucht er sich als ein Gebrauchter
So muß man stehen zu sich und sehr neben sich und will nicht zynisch
Werden, denn Zynismus ist eine scharfe Waffe, die entgleitet oder fetzt

9

A person who has done something to himself and others. I want to be dumb
And very shallow, I think of it as child's play, do not think poorly of myself
Yet here is some perspective: Go and go and fight and turn on a combat
Machine like before, keep at it in the best light in unanimity
With a cold future on the table, one does not die from the future
One dies from insobriety, the ability to lose one's head when
Needed, one does not die from an injured foot, from pigheadedness
Perhaps, one dies from deathly sadness which occurs, which never occurs
Predictably. Thus Philoctetes must stand upright, wait, if he falls, when
He is needed, he is needed, he is in need of himself as one who is utilized
So one must stand up for oneself and very close to oneself and not wish
To become cynical, for cynicism is a sharp weapon which slips or shreds

10

In fremde Leiber oder in sensible, feingewebte Seelen, geschehen ist's
Oder nicht, der Körper denkt, der Fuß ist schwer, ist eine Last, die
Nicht zu übersehen. Du fragst Odysseus, wozu der neue Kampf denn
Du fragst dich selbst, warum du wieder eingreifen mußt, du fragst
Geschichte antwortet nicht, und du bist selber stumm, und nur die Wunde
Spricht so rätselhaft, daß du nicht weißt: bleibst du verwundet schmerz=
Verzerrt: wie willst du altern, ein gedörrter Fisch auf trockenem Land
Willst du dich sehen, eingeklemmt in eine Einheitsfront des Überlebens
Willst du das Kollektiv? Die, mit denen du aufgebrochen, die dich ließen
Auf einem Strand ganz unverwandt und jetzt wieder angewandt, was
Damals unbekannt, daß Schmerz ein Mittel ist, etwas zu verstehen, das
Leider ohne Worte, ohne Namen, das leider nie in einem fremden Leib

10

Into foreign bodies or sensitive, finely woven souls, it has occurred
Or not, the body is thinking, my foot is heavy, is a burden,
Not to be overlooked. You ask Odysseus what the new battle is for
You are wondering yourself why you must join in again, you are asking
History does not answer, and you yourself are mute, and only the wound
Speaks so mysteriously that you do not know: do you remain wounded
Contorted in pain: how do you want to age, a dried-up fish on dry land
Do you want to see yourself jammed into a unified front of survival
Do you want the collective? Those with whom you decamped, who left you
On a beach completely disconnected and now once again connected, which
At that time unknown that pain is a means of understanding something that
Sadly without words, without name, that sadly never in a foreign body

11

Zu Hause wirst du niemals sein mehr, Philoktet, zu Hause war der
Ausgelebte Schmerz, die Waffen ruhn nie mehr, der Schmerz ein
Zeichen: ist er getilgt, ist Kampf auf Dauer angesagt in dem endlich
Angekündigten Ruhm, die Ehrenhalle dekorierter Männlichkeit, da
Willst du hin, wirst du hingeschoben, und sei's in einem Rollstuhl
Von dir selbst, du bist die Waffe, die Achilles' Sohn abholen sollte
Hast du gezögert oder hast du das Zögern vorgespielt in einer Geste
Du bist dein eigenes Geschütz, kennst die Trefferquote und das Glück
Ein treffendes Wort, das sich im Satz entzündet, wer kämpft, wiederholt
Explosion Entladung und Enthemmung, Schlächter, aus dem Tod rinnt
In einer schwarzen Spur ein Pfad, den Spätere angespornt, angelockt
Begehen, wie eine Kletterpartie in Zeit und Raum und Rausch begehen.

11

You will never be home again, Philoctetes, home was the
Pain endured, the weapons'll never rest again, the pain a
Sign: is it erased, is battle permanently declared in the finally
Pronounced glory, the hall of fame for decorated masculinity, there
You want to go, will you be pushed there, and even in a wheelchair
By yourself, you are the weapon that Achilles' son ought to fetch
Did you hesitate or did you simulate hesitation as a gesture
You are your own cannon, know the number of hits and happiness
A fitting word that ignites in a sentence, he who fights, repeats
Explosion discharge and disinhibition, butcher from whom death flows
On a black track a pathway that later ones spurred, allured
Treading like a climbing tour treads in time and space and frenzy.

12

Gehst du fort aus Lemnos, spitzt du deinen Pfeil, bist du versehrt
Und ausgehungert und verkehrt, daß etwas kommt, wie du erwartet
Vielleicht nicht mehr, du willst historisch sein und angestrahlt
Philoktet, ein beinah Amputierter, ein noch gerade Begehrter, der
Sich selbst ins Spiel bringt, zweifelnd, zögernd, ehe Geier kommen
Bringer eines Preises fürs standhafte Überleben ohne Erinnerung
Spürt nie die Spur, die Insel schwankt, die Geschichte ruft, es schufen
Kriegswucherungen ein unbekanntes Feld, auf dem zu schreiben ist
Auf dem zu graben nach den Schädeln, den Gebeinen, den toten
Geiern auch, den abgelegten, schmutzigen Verbänden, dem Verenden
Ich werde wiederkommen, werd zu den Waffen greifen, ich werde
Wieder töten, wenn man mich braucht, mich läßt, ich will nicht lernen.

12

Are you leaving Lemnos, are you sharpening your arrow, are you maimed
And ravenous and perverse that something is coming like you expected
Perhaps no longer, you want to be historic and in the spotlight
Philoctetes, nearly an amputee, one desired even now who
Brings himself forth, doubting, hesitating, before vultures come
Bearing a prize for steadfast survival without memory
Never sensing the track, the island is swaying, history is calling, tumors
Of war were creating an unknown field upon which is to be written
Upon which is to be dug after the skulls, the bones, the dead
Vultures too, the discarded, dirty bandages, the perishing
I will come again, will take back up the weapons, I will
Kill again when I am needed, am allowed, I do not want to learn.

XII

Simulation

Heimkehrumkehr

Ich werde zurückkehren, mit Gliedern aus Eisen, mit dunkler Haut, mit wilden Augen: Beim Anblick meiner Fratze wird man glauben, ich gehöre zur Rasse der Starken. Ich werde Gold haben: Ich werde nichts tun und brutal sein. Die Frauen pflegen solche wilden Kranken, die aus den Tropen zurückkehren.

Arthur Rimbaud

XII

Simulation

Homecoming conversion

I will return with limbs of iron, with dark skin, with wild eyes: at the sight of my hideous face people will think I belong to the race of the strong. I will have gold: I will do nothing and be brutal. Women look after such wild sick men who return from the tropics.

Arthur Rimbaud

1

Wo früher die kugelsichere Weste ummantelte, klebt nun
Die Creditcard in der Brusttasche des verschwitzten Hemdes

Dazwischen ein Langstreckenflug und eine sanfte Landung
Wir sind Heldendarsteller, verabschiedet, schlüpfen in Anzüge

Von Bankangestellten. Summen, die früher die Toten zählten
Sind an Zinssätze gekoppelt, Kids lümmeln mit Plastikpistolen

Stellungskrieg des Normalen; Hausbaukredite im freien Fall
Rasende Kopfschmerzen nachts, wir träumen von Rinderherden

Mit Stricken aneinandergefesselte Tiere, die wir für Feinde hielten
Niedergemetzelt im Irrtum, sie griffen uns an, wie wir ihnen contra

Wenn Aias schrie am Morgen ai, ai, als wäre sein Name ein Schmerz
Sind wir Aias, Mörder: schuldig und ruhiggestellt durch Tranquilizer.

1

Where once the bulletproof vest sheathed, the credit card
Now sticks to the breast pocket of the sweaty shirt

In between a long-distance flight and a gentle landing
We are hero-impersonators, departed, slipping into suits

Of bank employees. Numbers which previously counted the dead
Are linked to interest rates, kids are roughhousing with toy guns

Static warfare for the normal; home construction loans in free fall
Raging headaches at night, we dream about herds of cattle

Animals bound together with cords that we believe are foes
Massacred by mistake, they attacked us, like us versus them

When Ajax screamed ay, ay, in the morning, as if his name were pain
We are Ajax, murderers: guilty and sedated with tranquilizers.

2

Wir packen unsere Helme in gepolsterte Schachteln, solche wie
Die, in denen man weiche Damenhüte aufbewahrt, mit Traggurten

Und einer Beschriftung, Dienstgrad darauf, was Männlichkeit heißt
Platzt auf, Sex ist Politik, bündige Kostümproben im Wetterfesten

Wir treten auf in Fliegerjacken, breiter Schritt, den wir nie wieder
Ablegen (sicherheitshalber), wir sind bedenkenswert einig mit uns

Und der gebrechlichen Ordnung der Welt, die wir auf den Kopf
Zu stellen angetreten sind, haben unsere Birne aus der Schlinge

Gezogen und unsere Knochen gerettet, die kostbarer als solche
Die im Sand modern (so kommt es uns vor). Die Rettung Erwählter

Gut Ausgestatteter, „warum wir" ist wie kein Wunder, eher Zweck
Unter der Bedingung, daß Vergleiche sich niemals wiederholen.

2

We are packing our helmets into padded boxes, ones like
Those in which soft women's hats are stored, with straps

And an inscription, rank on top, that which is masculinity bursts forth
Sex is politics, compulsory dress rehearsals in weatherproofing

We go onstage in flight jackets, broad stride that we'll never again
Discard (as a precaution), we are strangely at one with ourselves

And the fragile order of the world for which we fell in line
In order to turn on its head, have saved our own noggins

And spared our bones which are more precious than those
Moldering in the sand (so it seems to us). The redemption of chosen ones

Of well-equipped ones, "why us" is like no wonder, rather intention
On condition that comparisons do not recur under any circumstances.

3

Und wer grübe sie denn aus, wenn wir träumen, grübe im Sand
Wo wir nicht waren, und wer grübe, wo wir vielleicht gewesen

Und wer grübe im Sand, wo jetzt die Panzer, schweres Geschütz
Und wer grübe im Sand, ob vielleicht ein Wort, ein Fetzen von

Wortlosigkeit eine Spur ließ verrottend, wer grübe denn wirklich
Wo eine Leine Feuer fing oder sich in einem Ast verwickelte

Und waren wir nicht zufällig unverwundet, wo wir nicht waren
Aber wir rannten doch auf dem Rollfeld unter den Rotorblättern

War das nicht gestern noch, wollten wir nicht ein Verdienstkreuz
Angeheftet oder nicht, aber wir waren doch glücklich gelandet

Unter dem Motorengeknatter Blätterdächer unsicherer Schutz
Waren wir nicht eben auf Suche nach einem Ort mit einer Frau

equally ashamed

3

And who would dig them up if we're dreaming, would dig in the sand
Where we were not, and who would dig where perhaps we've been

And who would dig in the sand where the tanks, now heavy artillery
And who would dig in the sand if perhaps a word, a scrap of

Wordlessness left a trace rotting, who would really dig
Where a line caught fire or became ensnarled in a branch

And were we not accidentally unscathed where we were not
But yet we ran on the tarmac beneath the rotor blades

Wasn't that just yesterday, didn't we want a service cross
Pinned on or not, and yet we had landed safely

Under the rattle of engines leaf roofs unsafe protection
Weren't we just now in search of a place with a woman

equally ashamed

4

Wäre es möglich, in sich selbst zu graben, fände man Laub
Stoffreste oder Holzwolle, Müll, Füllung eines Teddybären

Gedärm und den Faden einer Schnürsenkelgeschichte, der
Abgerissen, wäre es möglich, sich einer Hosentasche gleich

Umzustülpen in großer Erwartung, was wäre darin: Tabakkrümel
Flusen des abgetragenen Pullovers, zerknäueltes Sacktuch, Sekret

Ein Hornstoß, ein Ghetto kasernierter Testikelverzückung
Bückte man sich tiefer, verlöre man beinah das Gleichgewicht

Wäre es möglich, gewesenen Wald zu finden, lodernde Büsche
Wasser, in das stürzende Bäume fielen, knirschend totes Geäst

Auf dem später die Baumsägen heulten, rußige Splitter flogen
Wäre eine Wegmarke sichtbar: Hier warst du, hier war es zuende

Beinah.

4

If it were possible to dig into the self, one would find foliage
Remnants or wood-shavings, garbage, stuffing of a teddy bear

Intestines and the thread of a shoelace story which
Broke, if it were possible to turn the self inside out

Like a pants pocket in great anticipation of what were in it: tobacco crumbs
Lint balls of a worn sweater, wadded up pocket handkerchief, secretions

A bugle blast, a ghetto of barracked testicle ecstasy
If one stooped lower, one would nearly lose one's balance

If it were possible to find woods from before, bushes ablaze
Water into which toppling trees fell, creaking dead branches

Upon which the pruning saws later howled, sooty splinters flew
If a landmark were visible: Here you were, here it was over

All but.

5

Vollkommene Häuslichkeit, niederzudrückende Türklinken
Brummende Kühlgeräte, eine Glühbirne im Nu ausgetauscht

Frische Handtücher im Bad und eine frische Frau mit Fragen
In den Augen, die sie nicht ausspricht, nicht zu übersehen

Friedliches Summen und Zimmerspringbrunnen mit verläßlich
Wässrigem Ausstoß, überaus friedliche Rede am Kriegerdenkmal

Ein Gedenken, das die Denkenden ausschließt, Wetterfront, die
In den Knochen aufzieht, ein Wehtun, altertümliche Karottenblüte

Und wir sind da, in eine Starre gebannt, die uns selbst verwundert
Verwundet sind wir nicht, alles geht seinen Gang, Neonormalität

Der wir leidlich gewachsen, getestet belastbar, lehrreich war es
Im Dreck, im Betäubenden, aber wen lehren, der nicht im Sand

                              Seetüchtig geworden.

5

Perfect domesticity, door handles to be pressed down
Humming cooling devices, a light bulb changed in a flash

Fresh towels in the bath and a fresh woman with questions
In her eyes which she does not articulate, not to be missed

Peaceful buzzing and indoor fountains with dependably
Watery output, extremely peaceful speech at the war memorial

A remembrance which precludes those thinking, weather front which
Gathers in the bones, an aching, antiquarian carrot blossom

And we are there, spellbound in a numbness which amazes even us
We are not wounded, everything takes its course, neo-normalcy

Which we bore fairly well, proved resilient, it was instructive in the dirt
In the benumbing, but instruct whom, who didn't become seaworthy

In the sand.

6

Was wir gesehen, wollen wir nicht gesehen haben (blindlings)
Und wollen schlafen, traumhaft ausgeschlafen sein, retirieren

Die weiße Fläche des Gedächtnisses: ein Schneefeld durchpflügt
Erfrorenes Hirn. Auf Photos sind die Augen mit Balken unkenntlich

Unkenntlich sind wir uns selbst auf den Bildern in der Brieftasche
Wie glücklich könnten wir sein, ohne an Brände zu denken, die wir

Gelegt, an Töten und Getötetwerden (Luft und Boden) – dächten
An Rasenflächen und rollende Bälle, erleben wir zu viel oder wenig

Machen wir uns etwas vor oder sind wir aus Knochen gemacht
Die später vergraben werden und nur langsam vermodern oder

Stillgelegt das Hirn mit all seinen unnützen Gedanken, die Kinder
Haben den Hamster im Garten vergraben und Tulpen gepflanzt.

6

What we've seen, we don't want to have seen (blindly)
And want to sleep, to be dreamily well rested, to retire

The white expanse of memory: a snowfield is plowing through
Frostbitten brain. In photos our eyes are unrecognizable from black bars

We are unrecognizable even to ourselves in the pictures in the briefcase
How happy we could be, not thinking about fires that we

Set, about killing and being killed (air and ground) – we could think
About lawns and rolling balls, do we experience too much or too little

Are we fooling ourselves or are we made of bones
That will later be buried and only slowly decay or

Is the brain shut down with all its useless thoughts, the children
Have buried the hamster in the garden and planted tulips.

7

Sahen uns mit den blanken Augen der Welt, verkabelt mit
Allem, die Satellitenbilder schwebten über uns. Wir waren

Zufrieden mit unserem Sieg, der verdient schien auf lange
Sicht. Und wenn die Kinder fragten: Was hast du gemacht

Im Krieg, als andere über Gräber hinweg und im Graben
Verscharrt – : die Luft zum Schneiden und das Fenster gekippt

Als andere bluteten und wir manchmal heftiger oder nicht
Da räusperten wir uns sorgsam, griffen zum Glas, Eiswürfel

Klackerten, dämpften Erwartung, nein, nicht Vieh gemetzelt
Bilder waren in uns eingegangen, bis wir Bilder waren, die töteten

Blieben wir lebendig, Heimkehrer wie Sportler blumenumkränzt
Getöse von Müllautos in der Ferne. Und kraulten Hundeohren.

7

Saw ourselves with the bare eyes of the world, wired with
Everything, the satellite pictures hovered over us. We were

Content with our victory which seemed deserved in the long
Run. And whenever children asked: What did you do

In the war, when others were beyond the grave and buried in shallow
Graves – : the air thick enough to cut and the window ajar

When others bled and we at times more heavily or not
Then we cautiously cleared our throats, grabbed our glasses, ice cubes

Clattered, dampened expectations, no, no livestock slaughtered
Pictures had entered into us until we were pictures that killed

We stayed alive, returnees like athletes wreathed in flowers
The roar of garbage trucks in the distance. And stroked dog ears.

8

Wir hatten von Schlachten gehört, die Schlachtfeste gewesen
Gerötete Ausschweifung und feldgrau getünchte Säuberungen

Wollten an nichts teilgenommen haben, Teilhaber waren wir
Doch unwirklich neblig in Fallschirmseide verknotet, verknüllt

Unsicher abgestürzt und desorientiert, wo und wie wir gelandet
Niemals so schien es im Unwirtlichen, aber wir, die Geretteten

Waren unweigerlich ratlos. Leute zurrten an den Schnüren
Der Fallschirme, wollten aus den Fäden Socken stricken, ach

Die Armen, auch wir waren arm oder ärmer, weil die Fäden
An denen wir hingen und wir taumelten, rissen Schnüre nicht

Wußten nicht, wo ein Freund, wo Feind (Nähe durch Entfernung)
Wußten, wir waren zu Hause in Landungsnächten ein Traumverlust.

8

We had heard about battles that were butcher feasts
Reddened excess and field-gray whitewashed cleansings

Didn't want to have taken part in anything, we were participants
Yet surreally nebulously knotted, tangled in parachute silk

Crashed dangerously and disoriented, where and how we landed
Never did it appear so with the inhospitable, but we, the rescued ones

Were inevitably clueless. People lashed down the cords
Of the parachutes, wanted to knit socks from the threads, oh

The poor things, we too were poor or poorer because the threads
Upon which we hung and we tumbled, did not tear the laces

Didn't know where a friend, where foe (closeness through distance)
Knew we were at home in landing nights a loss of dreaming.

9

War ich ein Schläfer, der alles sah, sehen mußte und sehen wollte
Ich sah die Efeuranken und den wilden Wein, die Fensterkreuze

Schilfbestandene Ufer, ich sah die schlecht geflickten Dächer
Und schüttere Dornensträucher. Ich sah die Dunkelheit, sie kam

Aus allen Gassen und blieb überlang, sah ich die hungrigen Hunde
Mehr wie Hyänen, aber voller Gier, peilend die Augen, liderlos

Sah ich den zottigen Himmel und silbern ausgefranste Wolken
Ich war wie Wasser, durchlässig, war ein Regenwasservorhang

In der Nacht, als ich da saß und wachte, dachte an die Männer
Heimgekehrt, verstummt, und ich wachte an kleinen Monitoren

Das Wasser tropfte, Bilder frästen sich mir ein, sehend war ich
Blickbegabt wie Gott und wußte es, nur ängstlicher, erschütterbar

                                        Auch unsichtbar

9

Was I a sleeper who saw everything, had to see and wanted to see
I saw the ivy tendrils and the wild vine, the crossbars of the windows

Reed-filled shores, I saw the poorly patched roofs
And sparse thorn bushes. I saw the darkness, it came

From all alleys and stayed overlong, I saw the hungry dogs
More like hyenas, but full of greed, gauging the eyes, lidless

I saw the ragged sky and silvery tattered clouds
I was like water, transparent, was a rain water curtain

In the night when I sat there and watched, thought about the men
Returning home, silenced, and I watched on small monitors

Water dripped, pictures milled into my insides, seeing I was
Visually gifted like God and knew it, only more fearful, fragile

                              Also invisible

10

Geruch eines Bügeleisens auf nassem Tuch, Gestank aus Töpfen
In denen das Bratfett schwarz geworden, Ammoniak der Käsereste

Säcke für abgefallene Kastanienblätter, ganz ähnlich Leichensäcken
Und der Klingelton des Telefons ein getarnter Alarm, der schreckt

Ja, wir sind überempfindlich und unleidlich, als hätten wir gelitten
Nicht, der Wind knallt eine Tür ins Schloß, Ohrfeigen fürs Gehör

Die Nase wehrlos, als hätten wir nicht genug gerochen, und Hände
Baumeln, als fehlte ihnen eine Waffe oder der Griff eines Messers

Ausgebeulte Taschen verflachen, nichts darin und die Hände schlapp
Wir sehen mit den Nüstern und hören mit den Augen, was ist das

Dieser Turm aus polierten Kugeln, dampfend in der Goldrandschüssel
Sieht aus wie ein Berg Kanonenkugeln, und es sind nur Kartoffelklöße.

10

Smell of an iron on wet cloth, stench from pots in which
Cooking fat turned black, ammonia of cheese remnants

Sacks for fallen chestnut leaves, very similar to body bags
And the ring tone of the telephone a concealed alarm that startles

Yes, we are overly sensitive and unbearable, as if we hadn't
Suffered, the wind bangs a door shut, boxing the ears for hearing

The nose defenseless, as if we hadn't smelled enough, and hands
Dangling as if they were lacking a weapon or the handle of a knife

Baggy pockets flatten out, nothing inside and the hands limp
We see with our nostrils and hear with our eyes, what is that

This tower of polished balls, steaming in the gold-edged bowl
Looks like a pile of cannonballs and it is only potato dumplings.

11

Wie auf Ansichtskarten war der Friede erstarrt, mit einem Finger
Konnte man spazieren gehen auf der glänzenden Oberfläche, wir

Dachten, es wäre schön, an Schönes zu denken, an Küstenstraßen
Klippen, Schaumkronen, sahen uns selbst prustend im Wasser

Die Luftmatratze mit den sonnengelben Streifen, den Wasserball
Der Kinder, die Sand in einen Eimer schöpften und ausgossen

Immer wieder, als wäre Odysseus nie, wäre Philoktet auf dieser Insel
Das Blätterdach fiel uns ein, verbrannter Schatten, die Zweige ratsch

Und wir darüber in unserer Maschine Abrasierer, Kaputtmacher
Feuerbringer und Verlöscher, wo wir waren, war dann nichts mehr

Das wußten wir, wollten es nicht wissen, da war der Strand, Wellental
So blau, gischtschäumend, Schönheit blindlings in den Sand gesetzt

Verfügbar

11

Like on picture postcards peace stood still, with one finger
One could take a walk atop the gleaming surface area, we

Thought it would be nice to think about niceties, about coastal roads
Cliffs, white crests, saw ourselves snorting in the water

The air mattress with the sun-yellow stripes, the beach ball
Of the children who scooped and poured out sand with a pail

Again and again, as if Odysseus never were, Philoctetes were on this island
The leaf roof fell in on us, burnt shadow, branches skritch

And we above that in our machine eradicators, demolition experts
Fire-starters and extinguishers, wherever we were, there was nothing anymore

We knew that, didn't want to know it, the beach was there, wave
Trough so blue, spray-foaming, beauty blindly placed in the sand

                                        At our disposal

12

Wäre ein Versuch, nicht zur Deckung zu kommen, Geschichte
Wäre ein Versuch gewesen, der Abhängigkeit zu entkommen

Dies wäre vermutlich ein untauglicher Versuch, wie jemand den
Finger hebt, linkshändig beschämt, den Wind prüfend, zunichte

Gemacht unvollkommen bei ausgeschalteten Motoren öffentlich
Aus den Augen, aus dem Sinn geschlagen, geradeaus Augen

Die blank & blau erfreulich weit und breit und fern zu sehen
Sich ermächtigt haben im überaus furchtlos Bedeckten, all das

War zu sehen und entging den Augen nicht, was überkreuz oder
Überkopf schwergängig lief: Wir waren nicht dazu da, den Kopf

Zu verstecken, vernünftig zu verrecken, das verstehen Sie auch
Der Sie hier unleugbar als Zeuge Flagge zeigen werden oder nicht.

12

Would an attempt not to take cover be history
Would an attempt have been to escape subjection

This would presumably be an unfit attempt, like someone
Lifting a finger, left-handedly ashamed, testing the wind, reduced

To nothing imperfectly with turned-off engines in public
Beaten out of sight, out of mind, eyes straight ahead

Bare & blue beautifully far and wide and distant in view
Have empowered themselves in the overly fearless cover, all that

Was in view and did not evade the eyes, that went awry or
Stiffly overhead: We were not there for the purpose of hiding

Our heads, of perishing sensibly, you understand that as well
Where you will undeniably show your colors here as witness or not.